# A ROOM — *in* — DODGE CITY

# ROOM
— in —
# DODGE CITY

*A Novel-in-Vignettes*

## David Leo Rice

Illustrations by
Christina Collins

Alternating Current
Boulder, Colorado

*A Room in Dodge City: A Novel-in-Vignettes*
David Leo Rice
©2017 Alternating Current Press

Alternating Current
Boulder, Colorado
alternatingcurrentarts.com

ISBN-10: 1-946580-00-7
ISBN-13: 978-1-946580-00-9
First Edition: February 2017

*For Ingrid and my parents,*
*with love.*

# ADVANCE *Praise*

"What might happen if Edvard Munch knew alt-folk, lived in the U.S., and decided to paint directly on the inside of his own skull rather than on canvas. A deeply odd book that still possesses enormous resonance."
— Brian Evenson, author of *A Collapse of Horses*,
*Windeye*, and ALA-RUSA Award-winner *Last Days*

"*A Room in Dodge City* is the beatific son who materialized from the thermals of a Lynchian desert and then drifted from town to town until finally doing time, only to be paroled on work release to save the world, not by changing your life so much as by readjusting your understanding of the life that you've been living. At the same time, Rice cares deeply about his characters, and this comes out in every vignette. He doesn't follow the nihilistic postmodern structure by declaring life as meaningless or hopeless. What we do find is the presence of hope in all things, no matter how rundown they might appear on the surface."
— Joe Halstead, author of *West Virginia*

"The writing is David Lynch meets Neil Gaiman meets Samuel Beckett and the Theater of the Absurd. Just as Dodge City is a place the narrator can never leave, Rice's book sucks you in and doesn't let you walk out of it intact, either."
— Nick Antosca, author of *The Girlfriend Game*,
*Midnight Picnic*, and *Fires*, and creator of SyFy's *Channel Zero*

"In *A Room in Dodge City*, David Leo Rice has made good on the promise of the disturbing forays into the surrealism of everyday life that are his short stories. Dodge City is a walk on the dark side of the contemporary imagination that reworks the post-realist storytellings of Donald Barthelme or Henri Michaux into a voice that is unique. A picaresque novel for the age of the Darknet and Tor."
— Simon Pummell, director of *Bodysong*,
*Shock Head Soul*, and *Identicals*

"Last night in Dodge City, the zeitgeist saw its doppelgänger. Last night in Dodge City, American culture committed suicide and its pineal gland pumped DMT into the water mains. With a draftsman's hand and a psychonaut's eye, David Leo Rice has mapped the alien precinct in which we already live. I've never encountered a book so strange yet so familiar. Writers such as William Burroughs and Samuel Delany may have helped prepare the ground, but this high-speed, controlled drift across it is all Rice's own."
— Joanna Ruocco, Pushcart Prize winner and
author of *Dan* and *A Compendium of Domestic Incidents*

"In his mind-boggling debut novel, Rice conjures a series of seemingly unassuming vignettes that read like a revelatory prose poem written by the Zodiac Killer—my favorite kind of literature. There's something to be said about masks and facemasks, but also, the character of the Night Crusher or, how Zodiac Killer wishes he were the Night Crusher. Wow! *A Room in Dodge City* is a celebration of what it means to know that you know that you can never know everything."

—Mike Kleine, author of *Kanley Stubrick*

"Don't enter into David Leo Rice's terrifying and hilarious fictional multiverse looking for causality, continuity, or logic, as we know them. Do, and never really leave. *A Room in Dodge City* will plunge you into a nightmarish warren-maze where somewhere, amid the numberless trapdoors, inner chambers, and branching halls on branching halls, a literary orgy is going down among the imaginative intellects of Blake Butler, Kathryn Davis, Haruki Murakami, Livia Llewellyn, and Robert Coover, refereed by Cronenberg and Lynch."

—Adrian Van Young, author of *Shadows in Summerland* and *The Man Who Noticed Everything*

"Unsettling and unsettled, reading David Leo Rice's *A Room in Dodge City* is like reading Jakob von Gunten's dream journal the day after he'd stayed up late to watch *High Plains Drifter* and *Videodrome*. An impossible mix of the antic and the sinister."

—Gabriel Blackwell, author of *Madeleine E.* and *The Natural Dissolution of Fleeting-Improvised-Men*

"Rice's *A Room in Dodge City* warps the serial format to its own uncanny ends. It begins with a stranger arriving in a new town, but that's the last conventional move in this spellbinding and cinematic novel. You'll soon encounter toilet crucifixes, suicide students, and rock stars on vacation from being dead. Briskly paced with elegantly streamlined prose, the book follows its own impeccably strange and addictive dream logic."

—Jeff Jackson, author of *Mira Corpora* and *Novi Sad*

"Like Dodge City itself, David Leo Rice's novel has a heart of infinite evil. Rice's imagination and wit make this journey into the deepest pits of hell much more fun than it should be. Readers shouldn't hesitate to book a room."

—John Dermot Woods, author of *The Baltimore Atrocities*

"*A Room in Dodge City* is a vivid, precisely described nightmare filled with jokes for people who think nothing is funny anymore. David Leo Rice imagines American pop culture as a Hieronymus Bosch painting come to life, and he gives us a carnival barker's tour through a disturbing landscape of lost souls, vain ambitions, and distorted identities, ultimately finding a path to redemption through the spiritual wreckage."

—Mark Beauregard, author of *The Whale: A Love Story*

One morning I woke up in a room in the nation's heart, and couldn't think for the life of me what I was doing, or where to start.
—Augie March,
"Addle Brains"

I'm so sorry … my spirit's rarely in my body … it wanders through the dry country … looking for a good place to rest.
—Sparklehorse,
"Hundreds of Sparrows"

# PROLOGUE:

## *Arrival in Dodge City*

**I**T'S 6 A.M. I'm lying on a bench in a Bus Station, the only traveler to have gotten off here, staring across the concourse at the shuttered café, imagining it open, myself outfitted with a coffee and two rubbery muffins alone at one of its tables, waiting for the bus that'll take me somewhere else.

I've given up on all the people and engagements in the last phase of my life in order to come here, just as, before that, I gave up on the previous set of people and engagements in order to go there, and before that, and before that …

After cashing out of the last situation, I have enough saved to lay low for a year or two, depending on the cheapness of life in this Town. Longer if I earn anything, as I sometimes end up doing. I've always lived like this, heading ever Westward, away from whatever places and people I've happened to come in contact with. This has, so far, seemed the only viable attitude to adopt toward being mortal, which I've been told I am.

So as to keep open the option of return, however, I always scrape together some Material from the places I used to live, mostly trash—old files, receipts, envelopes with addresses on them. A sort of homemade folklore, these documents serve as my way out if I get too deep into any city or Town I come to. Proof, when I need it, that there are other places. Or were, anyway.

The announcer rattles on overhead. Coins start falling into vending machines, candy into hands. People are lining up for the payphone. I fall asleep on my belly on my suitcase on the bench.

●

**I WAKE UP** with two hands in my front pockets, each squeezing one ball, massaging cancer into them.

It's sad to abandon the impression of both hands belonging to one person, though now I can see it isn't so. It makes me not want to wake up, back into the common space that dictates how things really are.

"We did this in order to help you," one says.

"We had to flip you in order to achieve it," says the other. "We almost lost you."

I thank them as they retract their hands.

It's past noon. On the TV by the Arrivals Board, they're getting ready to execute what looks like a teenager. I hurry out of the Station before they go through with it.

●

**NOW**, to find a Hotel with a weekly rate.

As it turns out, not too surprisingly, there's only one downtown, and the Motel 6 way up the Strip doesn't seem the place to start. So I cross the Town Square, where a few old people are feeding pigeons, and climb the stairs to the Hotel Lobby.

**THE PORTER HAS SHOWN** me to my Room. Check-in went well, unless I missed its undertones.

The Room, after the porter's gone, is perfect. Comparatively big and comfortable, and replete with hiding places for my Material: panels that peel up, compartments under the rug, safes, deep back sections of closet.

Planning to take a nap before I parcel out the pieces, a wet, soapy washcloth draped over my nose and mouth like an ether rag, I wonder if, at the Front Desk, they could tell exactly what I'd come here for and assigned me this Room accordingly, or if every Room in this Hotel is exactly the same, every guest just like me.

I can tell it's not a question I'm likely to make much headway on or probably even remember when I wake up.

●

**AT SOME POINT**, I wake up and hide my Material. Then I lie back down and listen as the fact of my arrival begins to seep from my Blood into my bones.

It sounds like a slow boil, the way a swarm of bees on sugar looks.

●

# PHASE I:

## Spring,

## Early Days

# I Meet Drifter Jim
## on His Way out of Town

**A**FTER HOURS of daytime sleep, I tramp barefoot into the hall for a pack of gum.

Scraping the vending machine's money-slot with my outstretched fingers, I notice a large man coming my way. I turn to meet him. He towers, a hawk-talon necklace around his neck and green leather boots sunk into the carpeting.

He introduces himself as Drifter Jim, claims he's killed one thousand men and sired one thousand sons here in Dodge City. I ask him if he feels he's broken even.

He laughs and shakes his head. "Not even close, young friend."

I wait for him to continue.

"Headed out," he continues. "Bus in two hours. Far as Denver and from there don't ask."

A look passes between us like we each understand that a changing of the guards is taking place, and that to mention it aloud would, rather than confirm our mutual understanding, leave us both empty-handed.

So I wish him well and return to my Room, to fall asleep with a mouthful of gum and the dream that I've replaced him.

# I Meet Big Pharmakos
## Rehearsing His Comedy Act

**T**HE NEXT MORNING I come downstairs after a first shower and shave—jaw sore from the gum I fell asleep chewing and swallowed at some point—eager to see about breakfast. The sound of my Material boiling has already fallen beneath my notice, mixed in with the pipes and the radiator.

I pause to let two guys wheeling a slot machine go by. I decide to follow them, see where they're wheeling it. They're wheeling it into a Function Room, through some frosted glass doors behind the Front Desk.

This must be where the breakfast buffet is held, but it looks like I missed it. I scan the walls for a clock but don't find one, and remember that in Casinos there aren't any.

The guys plug in the slot machine next to two others. It lights up and starts to warble for cash. Behind me, an amplified voice says, "And he says, 'For my third wish, I'd like for half my head to be an orange.'"

I turn around to see a giant wearing a white satin suit and alligator loafers standing on a low stage, rocking from one heel to another like he's waiting for some furious circus animal to be released and come running for his crotch.

He's so big the mic disappears inside his fist, the cord sticking out like the tail of a crushed rat.

"This a Casino?"

"Yup," he replies. "Whenever they wheel that shit in. Fine by me. I get to do my act, since people are in here and they have to listen. What else can they do, right? Except gamble."

I look him over. "What's your act?"

"Comedian. You know. Road-torment, highest of highs and lowest of lows, unmanning, degradation, dubious and truncated euphoria. That whole sort of thing."

He climbs down from the stage, still choking the mic. At the end of the cord's reach, he offers me his other hand. "Big Pharmakos. Some folks call me Big Pharma, but you don't look like the type."

I shrug and take his hand, which covers mine so that it disappears as thoroughly as the mic.

"I was the Main Pimp in this Hotel," he says. "Before The Dodge City Gene Pool became fully Porn-based. Still get a few Flesh-lovers once in a while, like Drifter Jim and … "

Letting my hand go, he pulls out a card, forks it over. It has a photo of a skeleton with a circle around the pelvic region, his email address written inside an arrow pointing at that circle.

I put it in my pocket.

As I leave, I hear him clearing his throat back on stage, simpering to an imaginary crowd: "Okay, okay, now where was I … So anyway, there's this other guy in the car, too, next to Orangehead, not the dead one, and not the living one, either, but the one that … "

# Professor Dalton's Speech:

# Convocation of Drifters

**S**UPINE IN MY ROOM, Room-Service breakfast polished off, I sleep through the day and the following night.

After the smoke of a few preliminary dreams has cleared, I see a body of water and the hooded shapes of Pilgrims.

I fall into step with them, skirting the shoreline, slowly coming to realize, or believe, that I'm really here, not dreaming. At the very least, it's the type of dream that occurs in a genuine dream-place, shared with others, not in the usual mess of images squirted into me alone. So that when we wake, we'll all agree on what happened and remember it accordingly.

As we process onward, I have the sense that we're all Drifters, everyone newly arrived, washed by a tide into Dodge City where we'll now be counted present, however tenuously and for however brief a time.

The air is warm, going on hot. Across the water, I see the lights of a city that just keeps growing. It becomes a heaving, sweaty Port, a place of foul and libidinous disembarkation. Ships are pulling into its harbor, and the path we follow toward it grows ever more crowded the closer we come.

In a brutish Holy Holy Holy kind of rhythm, they chant the name of Professor Barry Dalton. It takes a while to notice that I'm chanting along with them.

●

**WINDING AROUND** toward the Port, I am overcome by exhaustion. I see a bed of leaves and moss by the riverside, under a willow, and go toward it, thinking, I'll just sleep for fifteen minutes.

As I'm taking off my shoes in the moss, yawning, I consider the subject of Time. I'm still young, I reason, and have never known what it is not to be. As I stretch out on the moss, I picture myself as an old man, in a building somewhere in Town, in a chair with a blanket pulled up to my chin and a wool cap down over my ears, a cup of cool tea beside me, the bag in a little saucer beside it. Perhaps then, as I spend day after day poring over my life, backing toward its end, my only regret will be: why did I sleep for fifteen minutes when I was young?

●

**SO I CATCH UP** with the Pilgrims and follow them into the Port in the distance, resolving first into the Port of Dodge City and then just Dodge City itself, no longer a Port once we've arrived.

"Looks bigger from far away," I hear someone mutter, and I nod.

In the Town Square, we form a crowd beneath the platform upon which Professor Dalton stands.

"Welcome, Nameless Ones," he begins.

His voice is such that no one can be anywhere near it and maintain a single private thought. Not even packed in ice for later. All distraction, all inner randomness and diaspora, dries up. We're riveted, listening in arctic stasis.

I feel him excavating the Subterranean Architecture of Dodge City, revealing it for a moment so that we might know, even if we'll soon forget, the true nature of where we are. At the same time, I feel the structures of my former life, from all the places I passed through on my way here, being ground down to stock material and pushed into an expanse of unlit oily water on the Edge of Town.

I'm reduced to two ears glued to the sides of a bowl as he informs us that we are most welcome here, so long as we banish the thought of ever leaving.

# At the Bar with Big Pharmakos

**D**ALTON'S VOICE DRONES monotonously like cold waves against a Scottish coastline. All the heat is gone from the air, so when a trickle of consciousness spills back into me, I use it to wish that I had a thick traveler's coat, or that I'd never come here.

The thought that the opposite is truer—that I'll never leave—is so discomfiting that I hurry away from the Town Square, faster than the dispersing Drifters. The feeling of the shared dream carries with it a sense of violation, like we all got too close too quickly, so, for the rest of tonight at least, I'm hoping to avoid them.

I take the first backstreet I can find, running with my eyes almost closed until I dead-end with my face against a door. A strong arm grabs my wrist and pulls me back just as Big Pharmakos appears out of the darkness to say, "He's with me."

●

**SEEN FROM A FEW FEET AWAY**, the Bar is just a nail-stuck box on a stretch of Strip with nothing around it except a defunct Honda dealership and an insurance storefront. The Motel 6 sign lights the horizon like its name is VACANCY.

The Bouncer that strong-armed me is a heavyset older man in sweatpants and a sweatshirt, a shock of white hair drooped over his eyes. He sits on a stool with a fistful of what looks like lotto tickets with cash mixed in, mushing everything around in a bad pantomime of counting it.

Big Pharmakos whispers, "That's Gibbering Pete, Chief Bouncer. Likes to charge an entrance fee. Don't mind him. Unless I'm doing a set here ... "

●

**INSIDE**, we take our seats and order drinks with a hand signal. I try to ignore the obvious presence of other Drifters all around us, trusting they'll sink into the background as soon as I let them.

So here we are. I have a $20 bill in my shirt pocket, which I figure I'll lay on my coaster at the end of the night and hope for change. A basket of peanuts with the shells on comes our way. Up on the bandstand is a guy with an acoustic guitar and a harmonica that keeps slipping out of its neck holder and into his shirt. I never see him replace it, but it slips out several times.

He's playing either an extremely slow or an extremely long cover of John Prine's "Sabu Visits the Twin Cities Alone."

"Cheers," I say, looking at the dim liquid in my glass, yawning like I've already had a few.

Big Pharmakos is trying out a new joke, but I barely hear it because my attention is tied up in a man hunched over the bar in a sleek black jacket with silver hair down to his shoulders. I can't take my eyes off him. His head gets larger and smaller, like he's pumping out used thoughts and sucking in fresh ones in a kind of dialysis.

I begin to sweat, wondering how much thought he's liable to move in the course of a night, and how much his head can hold. I picture it seeping out of him like nerve gas and wonder how long we're going to be here, how far my $20 will go.

Though I've so far only seen him from a distance, I'm pretty sure the man is Professor Dalton, and I don't know if I want to be around when he opens his mouth.

I feel traumatized by his speech, cursed by it, like the extent of its impact on my nervous system will only become clear years down the line.

"Excuse me," I say to Big Pharmakos, getting down from my seat to look for the bathroom, finding I can barely walk as I pass the Dalton-figure.

# *I Encounter an In-Demand*

# *Crucifix in the Bathroom*

**W**HEN I GET to the bathroom, unisex, I hear a low whimpering through the door. I wait, with some fascination, by the coat rack.

A poster hangs at eye-level that says, simply, 'Professor Barry Dalton.' The bottom is frayed with tabs that read either 'Barry' or 'Dalton,' in a smaller size of the same font.

Cautiously, I tear one off, a 'Dalton.' I put it in my pocket, but then take it back out. I feel better with it in my hand, where I can see it.

●

**I EVENTUALLY NOTICE** that the bathroom door has been ajar all this time, so I push my way in.

Inside, I encounter a woman sitting on the lowered toilet seat drenched in sweat, panting and crossing herself in a frenzy with a gnarled Crucifix made of wire, nails, and what looks like hair, mingling with her hair, which gets caught in its crevices as she brings it fast and hard across her face, completing the motion time after time.

Some of her hair comes away easily, woven into the Crucifix, as if part of it were a wig, but only part. There appears to be some aquatic component to this Crucifix, as well, bits of reef and seaweed.

She stops crossing herself and looks at me, exasperatedly, holding the object between us. "There's a sign-up list at the bar," she says. "You put your name down with the bartender; then you get a turn to borrow it, fair and square."

For some reason, I tell her the bartender's gone home.

She looks incredulous, but then sighs and says, "Don't matter much, I suppose. You'd have to wait at least a year until your name came up. Everyone's in line." She hefts the Crucifix proudly, closing one eye to keep a sharp tendril from poking it out. "What's that you got there?" she asks, pointing to the strip of paper dangling between my fingers.

I'd forgotten I had it. I hold it up to her now, like the fortune from a fortune cookie.

"Dalton," she reads. "That's your ticket."

I stand there mute to see what she'll do next. She holds the Crucifix away from me, like she thinks I'm going to make a move for it. Then she gets up, with a squishy sweat sound as she peels herself off the plastic toilet seat, and opens a panel in the back wall, revealing a hallway.

"It's going on down there," she says. "Make sure you take the door marked 'Dalton,' not the one marked 'Barry.' You don't want a Bouncer situation."

She waits until I'm gone. I can hear her taking up the Crucifix again, worrying over lost time and blessing my limp, which starts to feel a little better.

# Along the Hallway,
## toward the Dalton Event

**I** **LEAVE** the Bar, carrying my 'Dalton.'

Bouncers in jeans and black T-shirts come out from under lit torches recessed in the walls and glide beside me in silence. I wonder if Gibbering Pete is their master. Perhaps he's gibbering at them now, through their earpieces.

Behind them, off to the sides, I hear water lapping and dripping. It's too dark, despite the torchlight, to tell if the Bouncers are wet or dry.

After ten or fifteen minutes, a hand grabs me between the shoulder blades and compels me into a side-chamber, a kind of nave. "You wait here," its voice grumbles, and is gone, sliding some rough-sounding panel shut, penning me in.

●

**A DIM LIGHT** buzzes on from somewhere in the ceiling. There's a small box on a tripod at one edge of the space, like a nickelodeon or a Peep Show. I put my eye to the viewfinder, adjusting my lashes.

Inside, an altercation transpires between two pale men in faintly striped shirts, almost like mimes, but neither their costumes nor their mannerisms is quite polished enough. The film is silent, but one man is clearly shouting at the other, spittle turning to steam on his lips. The other has more of a slow-burning quality, staring in silence as his enemy yells on and on, in a fit.

When he's had enough, the slow-burning man points an unhurried but very deliberate finger at his enemy, drawing it from left to right, aiming at the man's lips, as if to mime zipping them shut. But he aims too low, and his arm's too long: with that horizontal motion, he slits the other man's throat with the tip of his finger.

The slit man sputters and shakes like a protestor under a fire hose until he's so drenched in Blood his feet struggle to stay on the floor, and then he topples, and, for a moment, floats like there's a rope around his neck.

His murderer regards his fingertip curiously, then breathes a luxurious sigh of relief.

●

**THE FILM REPEATS**. I watch it one more time, then move on to another, this one with subtitles:

A girl goes into a hip neighborhood café early in the morning and, after waiting in line, is asked what she'd like for breakfast. "Warm beer, please," she says, to which the barista replies, "Certainly," and pours her a boiling coffee.

The girl takes a gigantic gulp, and her face is burned to a nub. Slowly, as she daubs it with a napkin, a hyena face grows out of the wreckage, like it was deemed, by the film's Director or by some trans-human force within the film itself, 'the best that could be salvaged.'

She dries the hyena face with the rest of the napkin, clutching it inexpertly with hyena paws. "How's your warm beer?" the barista asks, coyly, to which the hyena replies, "A bit chilly," and, cackling (The subtitles say 'cackling.'), departs.

●

**IN THE BACK CORNER** of this chamber, I find a commode stuffed with letters addressed to "Doctor" or "Professor" Dalton. Many look like they've been steamed open. I pick one up and slide out the letter inside. It's written in a handsome, modestly italicized cursive. It reads:

*9/19/99*

*Dear Professor Dalton,*

*I regret the length of time that has passed since last we've corresponded. I can only assume that a great deal has transpired in your life, most of it, I hope, of a salubrious and optimistic nature. I can mostly report the same for myself, although, as you may perhaps not know, I committed Suicide in the summer of 1990.*

*It was no tremendous thing, simply a task that had to be attended to and that I did not want hanging over me any longer. I would have written sooner, were I not such an inveterate procrastination-artist. Anyway, since my Suicide, I have resided in a space that is not altogether uncomfortable, though one could hardly call it grand. "One ought better not expect too much from these sorts of things," as they say, after all.*

*The space, which I think of as 'my flat' just for the fun of it, looks to have once been a station of some sort, a bus or train station, although there are no tracks to be seen. Whether it is some rendition of Heaven or Hell I cannot say. I have the impression that it is neither, but perhaps some decorator is still en route, and will see to it that the place is hung with more evocative decorations soon enough.*

*There is a newsstand with a rack of belletristic paperbacks, the majority of which I have by this point read. A few I was unable to complete, while others took me by surprise with their directness and intensity of expression. There is a food stall in one corner that serves items such as calzones and Hot Pockets. The women who work there wear hairnets and call me 'Joven.' They have at long last agreed to serve me coffee. There is a chronic shortage of paper napkins, but, with patience, we persevere.*

*I look forward to your reply.*

The signature has been redacted. I put it back in its steamed-open envelope and feel guilty, like I'm the one who steamed it open. Then the guilt subsides.

# I Meet the Boy Sparklehorse,
## on Vacation from the Dead

**I** **PRESS** further in, through an opening that leads to another hallway, following the smell of ice cream.

On the way, a kind of sadness at the immensity of Time overtakes me. I find that I can no longer remember how I came to Dodge City, nor why. Any story I generate, and I try a few, feels provisional, like I'm trying to convince a listener who long ago decided to believe nothing I say.

●

**I MAKE IT** to the ice cream shop. I think of it as the Indoor Ice Cream Shop, meaning that it's inside the same complex everything's been in since I came to the Bar with Big Pharmakos.

I bungle my order when my turn comes. Scanning the cramped interior for a place to sit and poking at the dish of ice cream I no longer want, my eyes come to rest on the only table with a free seat, a boy of eleven or twelve sitting on the other side.

I make my way over and ask the boy, who's humming quietly and dripping ice cream from a cracked sugar cone onto his lap, if I may share the table with him. He nods distractedly, looking me over with one big eye, the other turned away.

I don't say anything until the pressure of keeping silent grows unbearable. I break it by asking his name.

He hesitates, then replies, "Mark Linkous, of Sparklehorse fame. In Town on break from the Dead."

He says it like he's on summer vacation, staying with a fun uncle. I could be that fun uncle, I think.

Then I think of the Suicide Student who wrote to Professor Dalton, filing this interaction away in that category. And I think of Sparklehorse, the legendary surrealist folk singer who shot himself through the heart in Knoxville in the spring of 2010. Arguably my favorite musician of all time, and a large part of the reason I'm here, wandering the country rather than living stably in any one part of it.

"Sparklehorse is gone," he says, before I can formulate any of what I'm thinking into anything I might say. "But, for good behavior, he's allowed to come back sometimes. His grown-up body is, as you might imagine, hardly seaworthy at this point, if you'll pardon the metaphor, so they outfitted him back into his child one. They had to make do."

There's something canned-sounding about not only his voice but his use of words, as if they're all fixed phrases from which he cannot deviate, on penalty of being sent back early.

I picture the bodies of Suicides in a garage, lined up like rental cars, an agent walking up and down the rows to see which ones are available, and at what price.

"If you really are Sparklehorse," I say to him, "can I ask you about … "

But when I look up, he's gone. I look around for a napkin dispenser to mop up the leavings of the two ice creams, his and mine, both now dripping from the table onto the floor. When I've finished mopping, I see him through the window, waving to me from the street.

Waving back, I wonder how much vacation time he gets. Probably not much, I think, and then I wonder how much I'll get, when the time comes, if any.

# The Spa of the Lamb

**I LEAVE** through another door, which deposits me in the alley behind the Bar, where Big Pharmakos is standing in a smoking pose but not smoking. I put my unused 'Dalton' ticket in the ashtray-trashcan beside him, and yawn.

"Wanna thaw?" he asks.

I nod, glad for the company.

We cross a few parking lots to arrive at the YMCA, which, I learn, houses the Spa of the Lamb.

●

**INSIDE**, we strip and dive off the slippery tile floor into the first, largest pool, full of the Lukewarm Blood of the Lamb.

We bathe happily in here, diving deep under, almost to the point of drowning, then we break back through the semi-solid surface to gulp down Blood-tasting throatfuls of air, hearty as a holiday dinner, before diving under again.

When we've had enough, we heave ourselves out, and I follow Big Pharmakos into the Scraping Room, where Spa Attendants scour our hides raw with the Bones of the Lamb. Then they coddle and pamper our cheeks and raw chests with the Tongues of the Lamb, at once docile and sandpapery, whispering sweet nothings when they pass our ears.

We drink fizzy, slightly salty water with whole lemons squeezed in, reclining on chaise lounges, reflecting on the day as we cool our feet in gray-mottled troughs of the Brains of the Lamb.

An effigy sits propped in one of the chaise lounges, icepack goggles taut over its bald, pockmarked head. Someone has stretched a condom over its effigy cock.

"That there's Harry Crews," says Big Pharmakos. "Greatest Florida writer there ever was and Patron Saint of this Whole Town. Keeps our secrets secret and our Folklore flowing. Knowing he's out there turns us into what we'd otherwise only fear we always should've been."

He lovingly props up the effigy when it slumps forward in the heat, kissing its forehead for luck.

●

**AFTER THE DIZZY THUMPING** in my temples subsides, I make my way toward the next room, where the Hot Blood bubbles in a much smaller, deeper pool, its surface area only wide enough to accommodate one diver at a time.

"Go ahead," says Big Pharmakos, giving me a push.

Unable to tell if there's anyone below, I tumble in headfirst, a graceless and not fully intentional dive.

I plunge down and down as the Blood gets hotter. The liquid heaves with what feels like the rhythm of the Beating Heart of the Lamb, and I feel it sucking me deeper, like a reverse birth canal, overriding any instinct I might have to resurface before I drown.

# *In the Bone Room*
## *with the Silent Professor*

**I** **BLACK OUT** and come-to in a room made entirely of Bone: ceiling, floor, walls, banquet table, a Bone toilet behind a Bone curtain in one corner, with a roll of Bone toilet paper nearly used up and a coil of Boneshit in the bowl. The Blood tunnel I came through is only visible as a red dot in the center of the ceiling.

The pressure in here is high, like it's deep underwater, but I can breathe.

Now I'm alone with the Silent Professor. His face reminds me of Dalton's but is so silent—whereas Dalton's seems always to be speaking or about to speak—that it's impossible to tell how close the resemblance really is.

The table is entirely empty except for a cup of Bonewater that sits by the Silent Professor's right hand, near where his cufflink on that side scrapes the Bone tablecloth. He looks neither at the cup nor at me, and, for a moment, I can't tell if I'm actually in here with him or not. I try to think of where else I might be, and then I think, how long will I wait for the Lecture to begin? before realizing that his Lecture is surely silent and thus well underway.

I want to lie on a couch or at least take a seat at the table, but there's only the one chair, in which the Silent Professor sits and lectures and, I would venture to guess, in which he's been sitting and lecturing for quite some time.

So I take to pacing, smelling my lamby forearms and the backs of my lamby hands. I'm barefoot, and the Bone floor feels like butter on ice.

The Silent Professor doesn't follow me with his eyes, doesn't even seem to notice when I pass through his field of vision. I start to imagine a pole or spike connecting my body to his, keeping us at a fixed distance, like a moon in orbit.

A shudder comes from outside the room—construction work?—and a dusting of Bone chips falls. Thinking it's snow, I again forget the floor isn't ice, and I flash on myself in some-place familiar, like Vermont, which only magnifies my sense of estrangement, as my next, inevitable thought is: familiar from when? From what lifetime?

The Silent Professor shows no sign of ceasing, just as he's never shown any sign of beginning. He won't even look at his cup, or at his French cuffs and cufflinks. He isn't interested in any of this, apparently.

Still, I want to latch onto his Lecture in some way.

Another rattle comes from outside the room, and with it, the sound of something being drilled in.

Exhausted, I think, They're setting up the Lucian Freud Exhibit on the other side of the wall. I lie down on the Bone floor to picture it going up. I picture the paintings themselves, which start out resembling people I know before morphing into abstraction.

Now that I'm relaxed, I realize this has been the Silent Professor's theme all along.

# The Lucian Freud Exhibit
# at Dodge City High

**N**OW THAT I'VE RECEIVED his message, a panel of Bone shifts open. I pass through it, hearing nothing at all behind me, then turn to discover that the Silent Professor has followed me through, dragging the chair he'd been sitting on.

We emerge into the glaring lights of what must be the Gym at Dodge City High and begin making our way among tables laid out with fingerfood. There's a wine station, and a corner where people are drinking beers from a red cooler on wheels.

The Silent Professor stays near me, slouching in such a way that I can't see the chair he's sitting on. I keep trying to check behind him, but he keeps his front turned toward me, as if aware of my intentions and determined to thwart them.

Most of the paintings are of frogs, some of daffodils, one or two of what look like tonsils, and there's an extra-large one of those black and red candied raspberries. They are of about high-school quality.

Up near the ceiling hangs a banner so long that the two walls do nothing to pull it taut. It reads: 'Welcome to the Lucian Freud Exhibit,' but it's crinkled and sagging in such a way that it looks like: 'Welcome Lucian Freud.'

"Did you know he was really going to be here?" I turn and see Rigid Steve, local billionaire, and his financial adviser, Fiscal Steven, according to the nametags each wears pinned to his breast pocket.

"That's him, over there," says Rigid Steve, pointing across the room at a guy with his back turned to us, who looks like he may be a security guard. The Silent Professor, relaxing on his chair, does not follow the pointing finger, and I sort of envy his resolve, or apathy.

"He's Dead," I say, and then we all together look back at that security guard. "How did you get all these Lucian Freuds in here?" I ask Rigid Steve, trying to change the subject, however slightly.

"A truck overturned near the overpass out on U.S. 56, couple miles south of Town. Driver didn't survive. Some scavengers scooped 'em up."

"A Lucian Freud truck?"

"Fur coats," says Rigid Steve. "My mother remembers those days," he continues, misting up. He seems to have become entirely indifferent to the paintings, which, to be fair, don't inspire much serious reflection. "Whenever a fur coat truck overturned outside Dodge City, there'd be a huge glut of 'em. All the ladies would go down to the stores and grab 'em up. Then, for weeks, they'd all be wearing exactly the same coat. Whenever they went to Town, it'd be a whole scene, everyone arguing about whose day it was to wear it, you know? Good thing fur decays."

I leave Rigid Steve to tell the rest of his story. Walking away, I try to picture an overturned truck full of actual Lucian Freuds. Then I look back at the paintings on the wall. The one nearest me is of a pitcher of cream with some flies drinking coffee on a little island in its center.

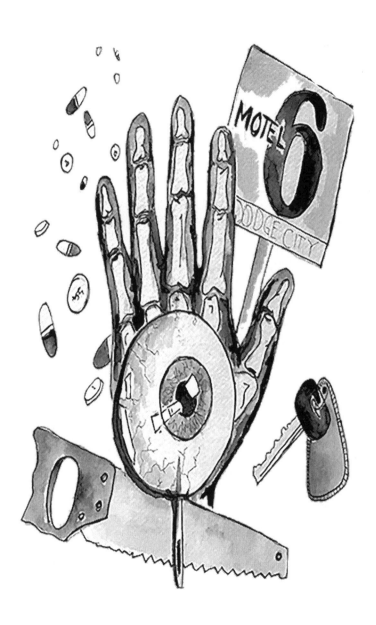

# PHASE II:

## Summer,
## the Night Crusher

# Gottfried Benn Ices the Party

**A** **STUPOR** of uncertain duration follows the Lucian Freud Exhibit. That was the biggest thing around here for a while.

I stay in my Room until a dust storm trips the Hotel's Evacuation System. "Everyone out! Everyone out!" shouts a mechanized voice, too loud to ignore.

So I comply, hurrying down through the Lobby and into the Town Square outside, where a procession is already underway. I join in, and am quickly swept out of Town, down a road I've never seen before.

We're all hurrying along the Arkansas River, heads hung low. There are Pilgrim figures on all sides, smudged together and multiplied by the yellow-gray air so that no part of my field of vision is unpopulated.

A gout of dust hits me full-on, and I stumble over something near the ground. After wiping my eyes, I look down and see it's a thick power cord. I run my fingers along its casing.

Big Pharmakos appears beside me. He looks a little off, but I know it's him. He can tell that I want to hear about this cord, so he says, "It's for circuses, when they come through. We got lots of inanimates 'round this part of the country. Inanimate Circuses, you know. It's so they can plug themselves in, get some juice. They plug it into their generator or whatever, come to life. Do their song and dance, unplug, end of story."

●

**WE ARRIVE** at a Diner where breakfast is served all around. It's a festive scene, everyone taking turns in the bathroom, washing off the gray dust that turns black with water as it swirls down the drain. There's a high spirit of refreshment, or a spirit of high refreshment, in the air, everyone tucking into plates of pancakes and French toast garnished with powdered sugar and orange wedges, the coffee rich, oily, plentiful.

Voices rise, everyone telling everyone about the confusions of the past period with a happy sense of waking up, collectively, or coming down from or off of something that had us in its grips for a while.

This is clearly a Dust Ritual, perhaps the only reason the Evacuation System went off.

●

**UNDER COVER** of all this comes a cloaked figure.

The bell on the door chimes as it closes behind him. Cool quiet then cold silence falls over the scene. Waitresses stop where they stand, holding their trays afloat, and the sizzling eggs on the griddle seize up, going hard without cooking through. I think of that power cord, imagine its having been yanked out.

People start tactfully but efficaciously leaving as the figure makes his slow way into the Diner's main interior. When he turns in my direction, I see it's Gottfried Benn, the German Expressionist poet.

He turns toward me, and I can feel the last remnants of mirth seeping out my fingertips and up from my chest, which now feels covered in cold vapor rub.

As he gets close, the hairs lining my spine stand up so straight they almost break free from my skin and rain down my back like staples. An old-timer at the next table leans over and whispers, "It's Gottfried Benn, son," as if I didn't know. "You have $60? He won't back off for anything less."

Just as Gottfried Benn gets to the edge of my table, his eyes narrowing, I reach into my wallet and, to my tremendous relief, find three 20s in there, like they'd been planted for this express purpose. I pull them out and press them into his Styrofoamy hand.

A moment of hesitation, then he turns, shuffles in his cloak to the cash register, and asks for change. Trying to avert her gaze from his, the cashier gives him six 10s, and he leaves the Diner, picking up a newspaper and a toothpick on his way out.

The air stays frozen. The old-timer leans across the booth again and whispers, "Don't get to thinking you won't see him again, son."

# Saga of Dead Hand and Industry Ed

**S**TILL SHAKEN from my encounter with Gottfried Benn, I'm skulking around near the Town Square, kicking litter and piles of dust now that the storm's settled, looking at what sticks to the toes of my sneakers, when Fiscal Steven walks by, dangling a rental car key from his outstretched index finger.

I can't focus right away. When I manage to, he's saying: " … And so I have my hands full getting everything ready. Putting the books in order, etc. He'll have questions that I'll want to have answers for, if you know what I'm saying. It'll take you something like half an hour, tops. I'll pay you, let's see"—he fumbles through his wallet—"$60?"

I picture Gottfried Benn coming back, and, thinking maybe a drive would do me well anyway, I accept. Over the years, I've done any number of daylong jobs for less.

Fiscal Steven hands me the key and is gone before I can ask him where the car is.

So I scope out a few, holding the key up to each one as if the grooves on the metal and the shape of the car might correspond in a way visible to the naked eye. Eventually, I read the license plate number printed on the rental car keychain, and get in the car that has that number on its actual plates, parked nearby.

●

**DRIVING TOWARD** the onramp to the highway, following signs for the airport, I pass kids and junkies huddled at one of the bus stops, frozen into a kind of folkloric tableau, like they're made of wood, posed behind a hand-painted sign reading, 'Geppetto's Workshop: Open to Visitors TH 11-2pm.'

As I drive, instead of turning on the radio, I say, "It's doing me well to take a drive."

Then I'm at the airport, drinking a Douwe Egberts, watching the luggage spill onto the carousel, empathizing with the people whose luggage will not arrive.

I'm holding a sign that reads, 'Industry Ed + Carla Ropes,' which I found propped in the backseat of the car.

After most of the concourse has cleared out, a red-faced, mustachioed man in khakis and a woman in a blue pantsuit wearing a straw hat come my way, and nod at the sign. I nod back.

Industry Ed holds his hand out to mine, and I reach for it, despite an instinct that, a moment from now, I'll wish I'd obeyed. When our hands make contact, I feel a coldness and a sharpness coursing from his fingertips to mine, and then down my palm to my wrist. The force of his grip spreads my bones apart like he thinks he's breaking up shrimp in a frozen block.

I moan, but Industry Ed is talking loud enough to drown me out. "Little trick I learned on the road," he gaffes, amicably I suppose.

My hand is turning yellow and foamy, and then the yellow starts to bleed out, leaving a grayish clearness in its place. I can see the bones now, shrimp-like and veiny. The fingers have swollen in circumference and shrunken in length, so that their overall mass may have been conserved.

"What's your name, anyways?" asks Industry Ed. "Dead Hand?" He laughs so loud that others in the luggage area turn to look, some of them beginning to laugh, as well. Carla Ropes rolls her eyes in a wide loop. I see that I've spilled my Douwe Egberts, and someone is now mopping it up, kneeling before us.

Both of them seem put off that I haven't offered to take their luggage, but, as I'm using one hand to cradle the other, I can't do much but lead the way to the car.

●

**NOW I'M DRIVING**, one hand in my lap, the other on the wheel. Industry Ed's up front and Carla Ropes is in back, looking through files in her briefcase. I notice there are giant 'Welcome Home, Industry Ed!' signs all along the highway leading into Town.

"Every Town thinks I'm from it!" he chuckles, watching with amusement as I try to drive in my current state. "What do you do for fun around here, Dead Hand?"

When I mention the Bar, he says, "Take us straight there."

●

**I END UP** spending most of the night with them in the Bar. Each time, to growing audiences, he tells the story of how he went to meet me at the airport and, when I arrived, he witnessed the disaster that had befallen my hand.

"Poor Dead Hand," he says, shaking his head. "Something weird clearly happened to him on the way to pick me up. He might have lost both if not for me. Let's show him how we take care of our afflicted here in Dodge City!"

Rounds of toasts compound one another, until most of the available bottles are empty. "Welcome to Dodge City, Dead Hand!" everyone chants, none louder than Industry Ed, a native son if ever there was one. Just before passing out, I think, This must be the tack he takes in every Town, ingratiating himself for the sake of whatever Industry he's in.

# Work Camp

**I** SPEND the early summer in the hospital, receiving one treatment after another, racking up a bill that, having no health insurance, I don't want to picture how I'll begin to pay.

By July, the doctors have decided that the problem with my Dead Hand is not that it's sick or injured but that it's a Criminal Hand, a Hand of Lapsed Judgment and Craven Character, and must, therefore, be transferred from the hospital into the penal system, its host along with it. Luckily for me, my bill gets lost in the process.

"So that's what's wrong with you!" exclaims Industry Ed, as if that'd been his suspicion all along and he just, out of decency, didn't want to be the first to say it.

A Priest of the High Hand is called to my bedside, like I'm dying. After the necessary ministrations and histrionics, he explains that my Hand is spiritually, not physically, Dead, and thus rather than more surgery or injections, what it needs is a chance to strive to articulate its better self and reach, as Hands are intrinsically wont to do, for the Outstretched Hand of God.

●

**SO I GET TRANSFERRED** to a real ol' time Workin'-on-the-Chain-Gang scene, an Alan Lomax lookalike standing in a corner with his tape recorder listening to us sing, or to the others sing, since I'm new here and don't know the words.

This is more steady employment than I've had in—I'd estimate—a solid ten years. It makes me uneasy, the thought of having to show up at the same place at the same time every day, for a fixed number of dollars.

Still, for the moment, I see no alternative, and I know it's generous of them to pay me at all.

●

**NEXT MORNING** we're in our dormitory, waiting for our work assignments. It was a military style eat-all-you-can-in-5-minutes breakfast buffet, during which I managed only to un-wrap a bran muffin and was then distracted by wiping the grease on my pants when I should've been choking it down.

I keep trying to hide my Dead Hand in my pocket, but our jumpsuits have none, so it looks like I have a tic, scratching at my waist the way a cow flicks its tail at flies.

The Foreman or Warden rides up in a cart and gets out, begins to yell. Since I'm the new guy, I get last pick of work for the day. By the time my turn comes around, everything's taken except reading aloud the complete works of someone called Little Søren in a free Mental Stimulus Seminar at the Mall, or else helping haul in some Mythos from another Town.

●

**HAVING CHOSEN** the latter, I get in a van with the Mythos Crew, and we head down dusty backroads, the sun blazing something furious overhead. The Driver lets us out next to a big, parked trailer, about the size of an industrial shipping container, if I'm not mistaken about their size.

On the side is painted: LAZY EYE MYTHOS. Chains and shackles are attached all over, and the other guys get right to it, grabbing hold of one shackle apiece. I grab the last one, in the back left corner.

I can hear something gelatinous squishing around inside, and allow my mind to fill with images of sedated circus animals starting to panic as the stagnant air thins. One of the guys bends down and fishes the circus extension cord out of the dust, plugging it into the back of the trailer. It starts to whir, idling.

With the shackles tight in my good hand, I start heaving when one of the other guys, apparently the Captain, gives the signal.

●

**WE HEAVE** through the afternoon, taking water breaks every half hour.

"So what are we actually doing here?" I ask during one such break.

The Captain looks at me, no doubt trying to determine the basic soundness of my mind. "Consolidating Mythos from another Town, just like the man this morning said."

A moment later, taking pity on me perhaps, he continues, "Lots of Towns out here, they don't got space for all their Mythos anymore. Gotta cut some corners, reel a few things in here and there. Focus on priorities. So they pack up their excess—like, whatever kind of stories usually take place in that Town, in the popular imagination and so forth—and send it to another Town, whoever will take it. In this case, Dodge City. So whatever Mythos is in this trailer—whatever Lazy Eye thing it happens to be this time, I honestly couldn't care less—will now, until further notice, take place not in that other Town, where it's taken place since time immemorial, but in Dodge City. That's consolidation," he says, and nods that the water break's over.

# *Keeping an Eye on Lazy Eye*

**H**ALFWAY (or so I'd like to believe) to delivering the new Mythos trailer to the park in Dodge City where it's slated to reside, the extension cord finally comes loose from its distant power source.

We all stop, letting our shackles go.

I sit and scowl and spit in the grass like the others and curse our luck at having this malfunction so close to day's end. Someone asks if I have a copy of *A Feast of Snakes* by Harry Crews, and I say yes, but then don't give him anything, and he goes away. I feel my Dead Hand baking hard in the sun.

The heat strokes us almost tenderly as we take turns walking to the edge of one another's sight to urinate in the dust or just to look out at the endless steppe, and then come back, so someone else can take a turn.

When we've all gone a few times, the Captain decides it's time for a change.

"Whatever's in that trailer, it sounds none too happy. I don't imagine it's any cooler in there than out here." He pounds the metal edge with his fist and recoils like he's just touched an iron that someone left plugged in. "Let's draw straws for who gets to go in and see what's up with whatever's in there, and maybe give it some water or somehow cool it down or console it or whatever it needs. Agreed?"

The others grunt, "Sure."

The straw-drawing consists of the Captain looking at me, clearing his throat, and saying, "You."

I tongue my molars and scratch my nose, decide against mounting any opposition.

"Don't worry," he shouts as I'm climbing in. "We'll all be right outside, making sure nothing goes wrong. We got your peripheries."

The door locks with me inside.

●

**THEY WEREN'T KIDDING** when they called it a Mythos. Judging by the street I'm now walking down and the foreign smells in the air and the can of root beer that has a logo I've never seen before that I pick like a fruit out of a bush it's been jammed into, this is a whole new Town. Live oaks leer over the street as I walk, passing mailboxes whose numbers are all smudged out, like chalk erased with the heel of a palm.

I hear dogs barking from way off, but I don't see any.

A few streets later, I see a porchlight on. The night feels at once cool in the normal night way, and blazingly hot, due to the daylight just beyond the edges of the trailer. I hadn't realized it was dark until just now.

Now I'm right up near the light, and can see it's coming from a pastel-pink shotgun shack. I wonder if whoever's in there is expecting me.

I watch my hand knocking on the splintery door, and then I watch the door open, not in any polite response to my having knocked but just because I've pushed it open.

Inside, after my eyes have adjusted to the deeper murk, I see a giant veiny Eye floating in a bathtub with a stepladder next to it. A very put-upon, exhausted-looking man is busy preparing an oversized syringe, its needle the size of a small spire.

I take a moment. If there were a pitcher of iced tea with fresh lemon wedges and sponge cake set out on a particolored and freshly laundered cloth on the table, I would treat myself to a glass and a slice right now, no questions asked.

Next thing, this beleaguered man is holding out a towel to the Eye, and waiting for it to slop out of the tub, which looks to be full of an amber brine. The Eye wriggles into the towel and then around in it, drying off however much eyes are supposed to dry off, which I'd guess is not all the way.

Then the man brings the syringe over and positions it in what's clearly a very practiced manner at the bottom of the step-ladder, as the Eye heaves up the steps.

I must've missed something here because the Eye has already jumped and is now stuck straight and true on the needle, impaled through the pupil, quivering with the impact, then going still.

The man is wheeling a bed over, turning down the creamy sheets. He helps the Eye off the needle and into the bed. Muttering fretfully, he stands back to see if his master needs anything else.

The Eye's jellied white begins to throb and fill with images like an unclouding crystal ball. Swooning in the room's formaldehyde reek, these images suck me in, until they become my new environment.

# Enter Night Crusher
## and Unholy Family

**I**'M IN a very high, semi-soft bunk bed in a dormitory, where I can hear the other members of the work crew snoring and struggling to get comfortable.

Still numb from the fumes in the Eye's house, I over-luxuriate and end up paralyzed.

I can't move my head, so I stare out in the direction it's facing, at the other sleepers on my level.

I can just make out the sight of a door opening, a figure letting itself in. The Night Crusher. Tall, slim, jet-black with burning red eyes and the nubs of horns. As soon as he appears, he becomes all I can think about, like my consciousness is now a simple monitor for his activity.

I see him walking the rows of bunks, leaning in to whisper in the ears of my workmates, growing tall to reach those on the upper level and shrinking for those below, paralyzing them where they lie, perhaps killing them.

But I'm already paralyzed, so, when he reaches my bunk, we simply make eye contact. As I'm not moving, he knows there's nothing more he can do. He glares, fumes, and moves on, his red eyes glowing a dimmer orange.

●

AFTER A BLANK INTERLUDE, I see him back in the dressing room he must have come here from. He sits sunk in despond, doubting his purpose, while his Handlers rush about, surrounding him with sweets and juices with protruding straws and pillows and divans. None of this holds his attention.

The room has a fuse-like quality, one of tenterhooks. Morosely flipping channels like some traveling efficiency expert laid up in his 66th Motel 6 of the summer, the Night Crusher at last chances upon something that moves him: a new episode of *Unholy Family.*

His Handlers perceive a slight lift in his mood as they prepare his complex set of antidepressants, but are careful not to show that they've noticed the change for fear of tempting him to reverse it.

●

**ON *UNHOLY FAMILY*** there's a family trapped inside during a war. Bombs are exploding on the soundtrack and marauders and mercenaries and bats are clawing at the doors. The family shivers in fear and cold and hunger in their house, which, for whatever reason, is safe against violent incursion.

For a while—skipped over in fast montage—they do normal stranded family things like try to survive and keep their spirits up.

Then, this being *Unholy Family*, things change. Soon they're all naked and huddling in a giant tub, like a Jacuzzi shell that's long-since lost its water, their clothes lost in some obscure way to the war.

In this tub they start slowly and distractedly fucking, all of them in there together. It's not clear if they especially know or notice what they're doing.

For a while it's a fairly standard Incest-type scenario, but then something in their collective physiognomy comes undone. All of their mealy, sweaty skin, which had been writhing in a resigned but still sentient and discrete mass a few moments before, all arms and legs jutting out of a huddle of heads and middles, starts to become conjoined.

There's intermittent machinegun fire out the windows, to remind you of the context. The Night Crusher, despite himself, is riveted.

The bodies merge more and more, reducing themselves or itself from many things to one through some sweaty calculus that the show doesn't make any too clear. It's not even clear if many decades have passed in this montage, so that perhaps this is the product of generations of inbreeding here in the tub, or if it's happened all at once, through some rare logic of sex itself, from which there's now no pulling free.

The Night Crusher stares in boyish fascination at the entity now occupying the tub, a mass of hide and what looks like gelatin and a secreted liquid serving as a broth around it, bubbling up from pores and orifices of various kinds, then seeping down the drain. Through the translucence, several orange and black centers are visible, organs perhaps, palpitating beneath knotted whorls.

When a bomb detonates nearby, the jets of the Jacuzzi come on, stirring up all the fluid that's seeped out of the entity, spraying some of it back in.

●

A HANDLER STANDS behind the Night Crusher, ready to give him his antidepressants but afraid of pulling his attention off the screen. Finally, during a commercial break, cut after a shot of the entity struggling to reverse itself in the tub so as to take its weight off a blossoming bedsore, the Handler gets his attention and, with all the confidence of an apprentice lion tamer, hands the Night Crusher his antidepressants and leaps four feet backward, knocking himself silly on the edge of a cabinet.

The Night Crusher opens the suitcase in which his antidepressants travel, and examines them with his fingers, his mind elsewhere. He doesn't intend to use them just yet, only to feel their familiar and comforting surfaces. There are smooth ones, fuzzy ones, Velcro ones, slick ones like gemstones, unaccountably wet ones, sticky ones that his fingers recoil from, and cool ones that his fingers love. Each has its unique positive and negative ends, and its stretchy, bendy, ropey, and malleable aspects, to be molded and clipped, snapped, or wrapped together with others, to create whatever combination his depression calls for.

He closes the suitcase, looking forward to returning to the show to discover if the entity has managed to heave itself over in time to air its bedsore.

But when he looks back at the screen, the entity is gone. *Unholy Family* is over until next week. He sits in his folding chair with his antidepressant suitcase flat across his lap, staring at the empty screen, beyond which the war has perhaps ended, or turned silent, gone chemical.

He tries to swallow his disappointment before it turns wild, but it looms up in him. Opening the suitcase, he slides a long finger inside, feeling around for the nearest soft antidepressant, praying for the strength to get back to work.

# The Night Crusher in Action;
# My Fairy Godmother

**T**HE NIGHT CRUSHER is now ready for action. Forcing my spine to obey, I roll out of my bunk and onto the floor, scrambling hard, if clumsily, out of the dormitory, fairly certain he's coming back to try crushing me again.

As I run, two other members of the work crew join me. The rest are still paralyzed.

We run hard through the morning outside, past the defunct Lazy Eye trailer, and into a stand of trees, which thickens into a forest.

Without looking behind us, we know the Night Crusher is on our tail, biding his time while we run ourselves out. The air around us whistles and whines, and the whole forest feels haunted by his presence.

●

**ON THE FAR SIDE**, we see the Night Crusher approaching from the other direction, his cool walk somehow still faster than we can run.

Just as he comes within smelling distance, another player breaks onto the scene. It's a brown truck, like the kind used by UPS, rumbling down a hill toward us. As it approaches, I wave my Dead Hand and jump up and down like a marooned sailor who's spotted his first reconnaissance plane in five years.

The truck skids to a halt and we scramble in, the Night Crusher chomping just behind us as we slam and bolt the door.

I slump against my seat and try to catch my breath as an old woman calmly looks me over from behind the wheel, as if we'd arranged months ago for her to pick me up.

"Well," she says, "how ya been?"

I force a smile.

Unaware of or unperturbed by the Night Crusher's pounding, she drives on.

We drive all through the night, none of us speaking, as the pounding continues. The Night Crusher must have climbed onto the outcropping above the back wheels, or else he's following along at that cool walking pace of his, effortlessly keeping up with the speeding truck.

●

**IN THE MORNING**, we get out at her home, back on the Outskirts of Dodge City. It's modest but attractive, a few rooms and a front and back patio, the smell of things cooking and having been cooked. Her husband, a very old man named Henry, greets us, and asks how the trip was. We look over his shoulder at the Night Crusher standing just outside the window, watching us and the back of Henry's head.

Lunch is served, then, after a few hours, dinner, then dessert. We sit up talking and drinking tea, eating cherry-shaped chocolates from a big foil-laced box, a bottle of cinnamon liqueur in the center of the table, its label embellished with the amber-like globules of ancient spilled drops.

Then she shows us to our room, lit by the Night Crusher's eyes, which glow as they follow us from window to window. I get in the bed she's made for me, and my companions get in two unmade spare beds nearby.

We lie there all night, waiting for the moment when he reaches a hand under one of the windows, slides it open, lets himself in.

●

**BUT IT DOESN'T HAPPEN**. We wake up to birds chirping and sun, the smell of coffee and bacon. My first thought this morning isn't fear of the Night Crusher, but fear of ending up stranded in this house, with no exit strategy.

After breakfast, we explore the premises and discover a number of saws stashed in innocuous-looking places like the laundry hamper where we drop our dirty clothes.

I bring one of these into the kitchen and show it to Henry, asking if it's meant to be used against the Night Crusher.

"Against whom?" he asks, leaning in to hear better.

I point out the window.

"Ah," he says, and makes a gesture like I should hand him the saw, so I do.

He balances it across his shoulders, puts his shoes and cap on, and goes out onto the patio like he's heading off to work.

The Night Crusher kills him instantly.

The rest of the afternoon is spent sitting at the card table under the window, looking at the corpse and the Night Crusher standing above it, quiet and boring as a still life.

●

**LIKE SO**, it gets dim again.

Around dark, we hear windows opening and closing. We go from window to window, dragging saws, and see that it's the neighbors, opening them from the outside.

"Just thought you should know!" they shout. "The Night Crusher could get in here any damn time he pleases!"

When he's finished killing them all and dragging their bodies to the pile inaugurated by Henry this morning, he goes back to standing there, staring at us inside the house.

"Do you need anything else before bed?" the widow asks from another room, either oblivious to the carnage or somehow complicit in it.

The liqueur and cherries have been out and then put away, both mostly finished by now. "No ma'am!" I shout, lying down in clean pajamas with a saw against my chest, determined to make a run for it in the morning.

# The Pagan Dodge City

**I** SLEEP through the night, dreaming of nights in my childhood home when I'd gone to bed convinced the back door was open—no matter how many times I checked—and that murderers were streaming in by the hundreds, creeping single-file up the stairs, knives out ...

When I wake up, unscathed now as then, I remember that I've decided to leave. I get dressed before I can reconsider, stash my saw under my pillow—aware that it's useless aside from whatever comfort it provided me in the night—and sneak through the window without saying goodbye to my comrades.

I tell myself I'm ready to die if that's what's in store for me, but it isn't. The Night Crusher's gone, having abandoned the pile of bodies in the driveway. I picture him back in his dressing room, proud of what he accomplished, watching reruns of *Unholy Family* while he waits for this week's episode to air.

●

**AT THE BOTTOM** of the long driveway, I find myself staring at another idling vehicle while the sky opens up and a gray wall of summer rain spills out.

Out of this vehicle comes Big Pharmakos, in rubber boots and a whaling slicker. He's talking very quickly about *The Wicker Man*, which he's just seen. If he knows I've been away, he doesn't let on.

"What's the upshot?" I ask, after I've gotten into the passenger's seat.

"Well," he begins, "I think we need to go there."

"Where?"

"To the island. To Summerisle. To keep our Appointment with the Wicker Man."

I shiver at the thought of the cold journey, and the cold arrival, the impending Sacrifice.

"I sense," he continues, driving through a rain so thick it's like we're sailing, "a kinship between us and that place. I believe that Summerisle may be The Pagan Dodge City. Every city has its Pagan Analogue," he explains. "Every Christian city, at any rate, just like every Christian book. Dalton, for example, spent many years attempting to write *The Pagan Ulysses*, until it was convincingly demonstrated to him that *Ulysses* is its own Pagan Analogue. At least that's how he justified quitting the project."

He pauses and picks up, a moment later, "Summerisle won't look any different from Dodge City, but it will be. It will do us good to go there. It will help us gain perspective on the return of the Night Crusher. Perhaps the Wicker Man will come to our aide against him ... " Here he trails off again.

I get the sense he's been searching for The Pagan Dodge City all his life, and has now reached the point where he'll pursue any lead he comes across.

But I don't bring this up. It's not like I'd rather be alone by the side of the road right now.

**A COLD SALT WIND** laces through our skin as we recline in our seats, rocking in puddles deep enough to produce waves. We're pulling blankets around ourselves and trying to cushion our heads on our inner upper arms, trying to sleep while Talk Talk's "Ascension Day" plays on repeat in the background.

When we start driving again, I realize how unwell I am. My Dead Hand is reverting to normal, its Debt to Society apparently paid, but the reversion is painfully taxing the rest of my system.

All the meat of my sides is shot through with queasy terror. I imagine I'd taste like wrong-slaughtered beef if someone were to eat me now, which doesn't seem all that unlikely. I'll have to excrete it slowly, I think, up from my pores with each breath, until I deflate enough to breathe actual air again.

I picture myself like a squid swollen with black ink, trying to seethe it out onto a white mattress until the whole thing is stained through and I'm drained to a pale jelly in its center.

# An Emergency Stop in the City of Motel 6s

"**P**ULL OVER**," I groan, after we've driven in circles through the night and most of the next day.

Big Pharmakos does, on a stretch of highway beside an empty billboard. "Time to get back?" he asks, mournfully.

I nod.

So we start driving again, through rain that's now so thick it's conjuring a vision of the Port City I saw on my first night here, when Dalton made his Convocation Speech.

"It's like we're approaching the coast of Scotland," I say, trying to cheer Big Pharmakos up, but this only seems to remind him of the journey we failed to make.

"The Wicker Man waits unaccommodated," he moans, like this is the story of his life.

I don't answer. I'm wondering about my own accommodation, a bath and a bed and fire escape instructions on the back of a dead-bolted door. The vision of the Port City gets astonishingly big and bright through the windshield, though the rain makes it impossible to tell how close it is.

**FINALLY**, we arrive. The vehicle tips over, and we both swim out, fighting our way through the waves and onto the shore.

A row of Motel 6s flanks the harbor, arranged in a jagged sky-line whereby some are taller and grander than others, like relics from a century of foreign occupation.

We walk down alleys of Motel 6s and up hills of them, through flatlands and ghettos and suburbs, a factory quarter and what looks like a prison quarter, churches, a zoo, Motel 6s one and all. The night is fraught with humidity and insects. All the Motel 6 signs make different promises: Some have HBO and WiFi and Continental Breakfast and even a Heated Pool. Others offer, simply, "two beds."

People shuffle from one Motel 6 to another, heads down, hurrying like they're afraid of or late for something.

Cars are parked in poor parallel jobs along the curbs, and buses rush by, stirring up puddles. Digital price signs line the streets, fluctuating many times per minute.

Big Pharmakos gestures at the buses' destination marquees, which all read CITY OF SUPER 8s.

I laugh, then yawn, then look at a new passing bus.

"Let's walk from one Motel 6 to another and compare prices," I say, planning to spring for both of us.

Big Pharmakos hesitates, looking at all the Motel 6s he can see. Then he turns and says, "No. I'm gonna take the bus. I think I know someone there I can stay with."

●

**AS SOON AS HE'S GONE**, I run into the nearest Motel 6 and book a room, get inside, bolt the door, and drop the blinds.

# Through the Peephole

**I**N MY ROOM at the Motel 6, I put on the Motel 6 pajamas that were laid out for me in shrinkwrap on the bed.

My other clothes, the ones I came here in, are gone, tossed down a chute to some laundry inferno below.

Before trying to sleep, I put a quarter in a slot beside the bed, expecting it to begin vibrating. But what actually happens is that a Peephole opens in the headboard.

I look through it, into a small house, or a set made to look like one. The main part is a dim living room, minimally furnished.

There is a TV set and a man who appears to be a colonel, in a tight military T-shirt, naked from the waist down, at about half-mast. "You some kind of a fancy bitch, ain't you?" he shouts, perhaps at me, but not in my direction. His TV says this same phrase, again and again, so that either he is repeating it, or it him, or they have each chanced upon the phrase independently, through some coincidence.

This last possibility seems the least likely, for, when I take a closer look at the TV, I see that this same colonel is on the screen, also naked beneath his green jacket, leading what appears to be an exercise program consisting primarily of the phrase, "You some kind of a fancy bitch, ain't you?"

The man in the room before me shouts it again, and I see that the object he holds throttled in his hand is an appendage, perhaps one of his own. He grips it ferociously and gesticulates in a wide dripping arc at the screen, as if he believes it to be a remote control. Perhaps he has pulled it off himself just recently, in a moment of imprudence, though it is not his penis, or not his only one.

I can see that soon he will crush it to jelly in his fist.

●

**I LOOK** past him, further into the house. In the rooms that follow, I see a great many figures suspended on hooks. They are almost human but bloated tremendously, their chests and shoulders and thighs so engorged that words like 'slabs' or 'hocks' seem like understatements.

They remind me of the conjoined family that so fascinated the Night Crusher. I wonder if there's a corollary, but I can't tell because their faces are so obscured by meat, they barely peep out at all, like the faces of hermit crabs.

Then someone else appears, a masked man. He looks tired, like he hadn't planned on doing what he's about to do, but he can tell I'm watching, and so he has to.

He takes up a cleaver from a nearby table and, striding over to one such hanging body, hacks off a handful, whispering, "You some kind of a fancy bitch, ain't you?"

It comes away easily, with a few gentle strokes of the cleaver, the meat's inner fluids congealing into the consistency of a condiment.

He strolls from room to room, each one fuller than the last, carrying the cleaver with one hand, snacking with the other. My Peephole zooms and pivots to keep up with him.

When he tires of this, he seeks out an unoccupied hook and eases himself onto it, still holding the cleaver. He wiggles around until he manages to slot the tooth of the hook into a socket in his spine. Then he relaxes.

He brings the cleaver down onto his thigh and tears off a nice handful, which he raises to his lips, wrapped in denim like a tortilla shell, staring at me through the Peephole. "You some kind of a fancy bitch, ain't you?" I whisper, closing the peephole and flipping my pillows, marveling at how far I've come since last night.

# A Motel 6 Bible Buffet, a Murderer on Trial, and a Rooftop Journey in Motel 6 Pajamas

**A**KNOCK on the door wakes me up, and I thrill to think it must be Room Service, though, to the best of my knowledge, I haven't ordered any. Maybe a little something complimentary, or included in the price of the Peep Show.

I open up and, sure enough, a chef stands before me, pushing a cart laid out with a white tablecloth and a little gas burner and some bowls of oil and one of those ovoid carving knives you only see at roast-ham and build-an-omelet stations.

He eyes my Motel 6 pajamas approvingly, then pushes the cart inside and closes the door.

He takes the Gideon Bible out of its drawer under the phone by the bed and carries it gingerly, by one corner, back to his station, where he puts it on a slab and drizzles it with oil.

I come close to see what he's doing, but he waves me back with the knife, then starts cutting thin slices into the sopping maroon leather. He puckers up his mustache and breathes evenly as he examines his work, piling the filets he's cut so far on another part of the slab and sprinkling them with pepper and scallions.

"Redacting the Apocrypha?" I ask, trying to make conversation.

"Don'know no Moses," he says in a thick accent under his breath, without looking up. "Abr'ham, Isaac, Judas, Joe … no, no, no, no." He picks up a slice and bites a corner out of it, chewing thoughtfully, and checks something off on a Motel 6 instruction sheet, picking at his teeth.

I try to peer into the Bible, suspecting that some of the meat I saw through the Peephole may be nestled in there, but he won't let me look.

●

**WHEN I GET** the sense that his carving ministrations are an open-ended process and not one necessarily intended for my benefit, I decide to push the TV onto the roof and watch *Unholy Family* from up there, looking out at the city of Motel 6s until my head clears.

"You gotta do every room by dawn?" I ask, thinking to distract him as I go about unplugging the TV and getting it onto the roof, as if he'd otherwise try to stop me, but he doesn't say anything until, a few minutes later, when I'm most of the way out the window, he says, "Shoes," and kicks two meaty rubber slabs out from under the rolling buffet table.

My other shoes must have gone the way of my clothes, so I slip my feet gratefully into these squishy Motel 6 flip-flops, big and shapeless as kickboards, and resume climbing and carrying the TV onto the roof, looking back one last time to see him dismantling the Bible's binding and showering the loose, protruding threads with Tabasco.

●

**NOW COMES** a slapstick Sisyphus interlude as I keep trying to push the TV onto the roof, and it keeps sliding back down. I slip around in my new flip-flops like someone practicing pratfalls from a YouTube tutorial.

Once this interlude is over, I'm up here and the TV is not.

I sit on a high gable, smelling the still Port City air now that the rain's stopped, and watch a murder trial on another TV that I found waiting for me. I'm right in the nest of aerials and antennae, feeding the whole Motel 6, so the reception is impeccable, uncanny even.

This one's showing a man on trial for murdering "a number of people" with a shard of glass. I think he's the same man I saw through my Peephole, cutting up those hanging bodies, but I can't be sure because he was wearing a mask then and is clean-shaven and clear-eyed now.

The show's narrator repeats the phrase *a number of people* so often it starts to sound like the stock descriptor for people in a group, like *a pride of lions* or *a coven of witches*. Wow, I think, he murdered a whole number with a single shard.

The man's defense consists of shrieking, again and again, "I thought there were restrictions on glass! I thought there were restrictions on glass!"

His lawyer looks like he's loving every minute of this, pressing his thumb to his mouth in an effort to paste on an expression of composed seriousness.

Now the man's shrieking, "I thought glass was free! I thought glass was free!"

Finding the whole thing a little hysterical for my mood, I push the TV off the roof. It lands on top of the other. The sight of their innards oozing together makes me hungry, and I wish I'd eaten when I had the chance, though I'm still not sure if I ever did.

As the roof is now empty of stimulus, I decide it's a good time to start heading back toward Dodge City.

# Rooftop Journey past Rows of Rubbery Houses with Masked Men Inside

**S**CUTTLING ALONG the rooftops, out of the City of Motel 6s, is rough going at first.

Then it gets easier, evens out. I'm still up on the rooftops, but they seem lower now, and flatter, and there are trees and what feels like dirt, rabbits scampering away as I pass. I come to think of myself as 'back on the ground' until a row of houses on a plain way below puts things back in perspective.

I creep over to the edge and look off. I see they're translucent, glowing green from within. They look gummy, made of rubber or some rubbery sugar or glue compound.

Inside, what at first looked like plum pits turns out to be hulking, monstrous bodies, slowly stretching masks over their heads and standing in the green glow, ready to go out and start their night-work, summoned back to the Peepholes by guests like me.

Except they don't go. For as long as I can bear to look, they remain arrested in the process of pulling their masks on. Somehow, it's as if their masks are both on and not on at the same time, being pulled constantly lower on their heads without clicking into place, like a living GIF.

When I've had enough of this scene, I retreat from the edge and keep going, thinking that maybe they'll break free of the loop once they get their privacy back.

The terrain evens out again, and I'm back in the dirt, at actual ground level this time.

I sit down on the first bench I come to and draw my arms around me, surprised, as I often am, at how much colder the night can get as it goes along, even after the sun's been down for hours.

**NEAR THE OUTSKIRTS** of Dodge City, I pass through an encampment of broken-down cars and pickup trucks configured like the Great Depression. Radios are set up; people are cooking over irregular flames, eating from cans, reminiscing.

I enter among them, hungry, and sit on a block of wood, waiting to be handed a portion of beans and bread, though I know I don't deserve it the way they do.

Still, someone hands me a plate, and I eat and relax, looking around to notice how old they all are. Like really, really old. The oldest people I've ever seen.

They're good-looking, though. They look like Movie stars from every decade of the twentieth century, all lumped together, and, here and now, all equally old, preserved in an end-phase instead of dying, the way I've heard that old film reels are kept in salt mines in this part of the country.

I picture The Dodge City Film Industry excreting them in waves, swelling up from the center with younger and younger stars, pushing those of a certain age toward the edges, until they're so far gone they end up stranded. I wonder how long they've been out here, and if there's any next place they're headed, or if this is it, forever.

The thought makes me twitchy, so, when I've cleared my plate, I put it on the trash pile with the others, nod, and continue on my way.

# Someone's Stealing Big Pharmakos' Comedian Persona

**I**'VE MADE IT back to Town, still in my Motel 6 pajamas.

I'm on the sidewalk outside the Hotel, looking at the banks of windows, trying to remember which Room is mine.

When I'm fairly certain, I go into the Lobby and am approaching the Front Desk when a voice grumbles, "Ticket?"

I turn to see Gibbering Pete, Chief Bouncer, fingering a velvet rope in the doorway of the Casino. I shake my head no, but a crowd surging from behind me overwhelms him, and I find myself inside.

●

**AN USHER COMES OVER** and manhandles me into a seat like otherwise I wouldn't fit.

The interior is done up in a garish 1850s Parisian playhouse style straight out of Nerval. Once I've taken this in, sweeping the crowd in the dark, my gaze settles on the stage, where Big Pharmakos is doing his stand-up routine. The audience falls out of its seats whenever he hits a punchline, sagging sideways into the aisles in slow-mo like he's hit a cell-phone-operated detonator and blown the whole place to pieces.

"No, no, no, but really," he says, wiping sweat with his sleeve and hanging back on his heels, shoulders loose and rangy like a boxer's, "seriously, guys, the thing that really gets me is ... " And everyone climbs back into their seats, ready to be blown away again.

"So, this one time, I was in one of those, what do you call 'em, like a ... " he starts, letting them simmer down, pacing the stage, fingering the detonator, wrapping his hand almost all the way around the head of the mic, foreskin-style.

Then he hits it, so hard the verbal punchline is buried under its visual effect.

After the audience has flown into the aisle again, and again picked itself up, I settle into a spectating rhythm. Though he doesn't blow me out of my seat, I'm impressed with his progress as a Comedian since last I saw him, in this same room on my first full day here.

●

**THEN SOMETHING ELSE** happens: Big Pharmakos sits down in the empty seat beside me, fuming.

"You fucking believe this?"

I pause, trying to relax before leaping to conclusions, looking from the Big Pharmakos on stage to the Big Pharmakos beside me, and back and then back again.

I breathe, count up and down from ten, luxuriating in the impossibility of the situation before trying to address it. The dimensions of the room are such that I can't look directly at the Big Pharmakos on stage and at the one sitting beside me at the same time. I have to sweep from one to the other, losing direct sight of the first as soon as I lock onto the second.

This makes it hard to maintain complete certainty that both are in fact the same man.

"That fucker's stealing my shit," moans Big Pharmakos.

I open my mouth to respond just as another punchline detonates, and the audience is blown back into the aisles, the room going silent in that action-movie way that indicates the deafness that follows real explosions.

As they climb back into their seats yet again, Big Pharmakos continues, like maybe he talked right through the explosion, "—and not even just my jokes, man, but my whole deal. My shtick and vibe and delivery and floorwork, and ... and my whole basic way of seeming and being. Wholesale ripoff up there, and look at me now, jammed down into some seat next to you like some nobody off the street—no offense—and nobody'll believe that I— And who is that guy up there, anyway? How did it happen? He's the nobody, in real goddamn life if there still is such a thing, and I'm—"

*Boom.*

●

**DURING INTERMISSION**, a kid comes around with one of those snack trays hanging around his neck, selling what appear to be pretzels.

I get one, and one for Big Pharmakos, and the kid shimmies on to the next row, refusing to take my money ("Complimentary, complimentary," he mutters, in a put-on sounding accent.).

Holding the thing, I see it's not a pretzel but a big doughy hand, hardened butter bulging out at the knuckles.

I recoil, recognizing it as an effigy of my own Dead Hand. I break it open to find a note from Industry Ed. It says, "Celebrate the unveiling after the show! In the park, directly across the street! Cheers, I. Ed."

**HOLDING THE DOUGHY HAND**, which I saved through the second half of the comedy show, I stand in the park with Big Pharmakos, who's still fuming. The crowd from the show is out here, too.

Industry Ed is up on a platform, the kind that people running for Mayor shout from, and beside him is a figure of about his height with a pale sheet draped over it.

"As many of you are doubtless aware," he begins.

I see people to my right and left munching my Hand as Industry Ed goes on, "Not long ago we lost one of our own to the vague forces of adventure. He set out from our midst one night, as the story goes, and never returned. He is lost to us for good, it saddens me to report. Or," here he breaks into a grin, "or, I should say, *was* lost to us for good."

"I'm back!" I want to shout. "I'm right here!" But when I open my mouth, it feels stuffed with dough, and I gag.

"He was lost to us," Industry Ed strides over to the draped figure, "until ... " He unveils the figure, revealing a perfect copy of me, standing dutifully on a mat and smiling at the crowd. "Until now!" The crowd gets blasted to the sides the same way they did at the impostor's punchlines in the Casino.

Industry Ed whispers to me onstage, "Do you see what I see? Do you see him standing out there, in the crowd, glaring at us?"

"Where?" I ask, leaning toward him onstage to return the whisper, my back stiff and my kidneys about to fail.

He points, and I look carefully out over the crowd until I see me, standing toward the back with Big Pharmakos, the two of us alone among the giddy munching faces, soberly meditating on the doubleness of the things, the ineffable superimposition of Dodge City upon The Pagan Dodge City, ever-present beneath us yet impossible to isolate as such.

●

# PHASE III:

*Autumn,*

*the Inspector*

# *Apportioning the Suicide Cemetery*

**I** **MUST HAVE FAINTED** at Industry Ed's unveiling of the other me, because now I'm back in my Room, in bed amidst flower bouquets and other Get Well Soon paraphernalia. My Motel 6 pajamas are gone, and there's a Gap bag sitting on a chair.

There's also a grinning poster of Industry Ed holding the hand of someone off-screen taped to the wall, which I vow to use the first of my energy, as soon it returns, to rip down and ball up.

I sleep until a jackhammer outside my window wakes me. Not knowing if I have broken bones and ruptured organs, I creak out of bed and find that I can stand.

So here I am, standing, in stale boxers and undershirt, back in my Room. I turn ninety degrees, so as to try standing in a new direction, and then another ninety, and ninety more, and then I get bored, and hungry.

I find a breakfast-in-bed tray tipped over and spilled among my sheets, but the spill is such that I can rescue a few elements, such as bread, a mini jar of marmalade with a strip of fancy tape connecting the lid to the sides, and a few hair-inflected orange and apple slices.

Let's eat a little, I think. Then we'll have the strength to tear that poster down. It turns out we're right.

**AFTER SEVERAL MORE DAYS** pacing my Room, living off the remnants of this breakfast tray, which came with a few stapled pages from *A Feast of Snakes* in lieu of a newspaper, I again notice the jackhammer that's been going all this time.

I put on my new Gap clothes and saunter over to the window.

Once my eyes have adjusted, I can see that the view has changed since last I occupied this Room. Now, I see a few derelict stores and cafés, and, mainly, a big grassy expanse with a banner hanging over it that reads: DODGE CITY SUICIDE CEMETERY, OPENING VERY SOON.

I see people talking in a cluster by a couple of bulldozers near the center. A news crew is huddled around them, moving their mouths. So as to hear better, I turn on the TV in my Room.

"And, so," says the petite, shriveled-faced Proprietor, "while we haven't ironed out all the kinks yet, the martyrs will likely go there," he points in one direction, "while the overdoses and reckless motorcycle drivers will go there," he points in another direction. "The Suicide bombers and other deluded zealots, here," the camera follows his pointing finger, awkwardly zooming in on a pile of dirt, "while the disputed cases, the, er, 'maybes,' if you will, go over there. Oh, and the, we're calling them, the 'taken by angels in the dreamtime slash sham Suicides gone right,' all go over there."

"So you're apportioning the whole place, looks like, down to a fairly specific level, correct?" the interviewer asks him.

The Proprietor looks annoyed by the question, but nods and says, "Correct. I have campaigned on Dodge City's behalf—I don't know if you all appreciate—long and hard to have the Suicide Cemetery built here. Only one of its kind in the country. It could have been anywhere, and would have been elsewhere, had I not campaigned harder than anyone else to have it here. We've got some pretty high-profile Suicides in discussion. I shouldn't say too much, but the name of Sparklehorse has been floated behind closed doors. No promises, since the political entanglements when it comes to these things are a waking nightmare, but I'd like to say to whomever may be watching: don't rule it out."

# The Funeral of Harry Crews

**T**HIS **BROADCAST** is interrupted to bring news of the Death of Harry Crews, Notorious Florida Author and, as has been made abundantly clear to me by now, Patron Saint of Dodge City.

"Death is the explanation," says the broadcast, again and again, trying to drive it home.

"I know," I say, before turning it off.

●

**I LEAVE** my Room for the streets, dressed in my Gap outfit of middle-management khakis and a blue Oxford button-up. I feel my hairline receding as I cross the Lobby.

Everywhere I look, grief manifests itself in a free-for-all of spontaneous tattooing. Anyone who has ink and a sharp object is tattooing himself in the most ragged and pre-Biblical script imaginable: Words of praise and honor to Harry Crews upon their naked Flesh, devotionally burning themselves with cigarettes and cutting themselves with parts of bottles and cans.

"Want to shoot steroids to get ready?" a guy I met once at the Bar with Big Pharmakos asks me, standing in front of where I'm standing.

I nod, seeing he's already got the syringe prepped.

"You know *Body*, right? *Scar Lover*. I mean: Harry Crews ... " he trails off, seeming to feel the effects of the drug as he injects me.

We go on in a pretty hopped-up mood, as if it's Harry Crews' birth we're off to celebrate.

●

**THE STREETS SEETHE**. Our hearts are grunting, our shirts tight with sweat and weird patches of muscle bulging out like armor for our gut organs.

We can already smell and hear the snakes. Teenagers lurch past us, shirtless in loose pantaloons, vodka bottles sticking out of their waist-sashes like canteens at the start of a Death March.

"When did you first read *A Feast of Snakes*?" one asks the other.

"My second month in the womb," he answers, and they both cheer in a practiced call-and-response.

As we keep walking, I hear this question going back and forth all over. Everyone's chanting it, building group energy as we converge for the Main Event.

"When did you first read *A Feast of Snakes*?" the guy I'm walking with asks me.

I almost say, "When I was twenty-five," which is the truth, but I'm afraid he'll throttle me for blasphemy, so I respond, "My second month in the womb."

Now the throng is so deep we can't push any further in. The whole Town is here, everyone so huge on steroids it's like two Towns crowded into a square meant for one.

To my right I see six guys eating a car, their mouths raw and bloody with metal and beads of shatterproof glass, a line of mostly-naked cheerleaders dancing and whooping beside them, twirling a banner that reads: Harry Crews' Acclaimed Novel *Car*.

A man on fire dances on the other sideline until he meets another man on fire, and they collapse, amidst cheering, into a single burning mass.

●

**UP AHEAD** (We have to crane way over people standing in front of us.), we can see a hastily erected platform on the other side of a moat of snakes, so full that some rattlers and copper-heads are leaping out and biting the cheering people in the front lines. Trailers are parked along the edges of the Town Square, Outskirts people pressing barbells on rickety home-made benches, pounding beers, throwing footballs, and reverentially gut-stabbing one another.

Atop the platform stands a figure in a gold facemask that tapers to a sharp birdlike beak. The sun glints off its surface so that we can't look the High Priest directly in the eyes—an old Aztec tradition, I believe. I'm certain that under the mask is Professor Dalton.

He's shouting into the sunlight, but it's like the glint off the mask is obscuring his voice, as well, so I can only hear a grating in my ears.

Then a cry goes up from the crowd: "Today, Dodge City is Mystic, Georgia!" they shriek. "Today, Dodge City is Celebration, Florida!"

Someone tazes me, and I start chanting, too.

"Who will the first Sacrifice be?" shouts Dalton-under-the-mask. I expect him to pull a curved, jewel-hilted saber from his robes, but he just stands back with his arms up as hundreds dive into the snake pit.

As they fall, the rest of us push closer in, right up to the edge, to watch as the snakes peel the meat from them, then start pouring through their skeletons, which dry almost immediately in the relentless sun. I stand as close as I can and watch snakes thread in one eye socket and out another, looking for leavings before they fall, eventually, to eating snake.

I won't say the thought of hurling myself in doesn't cross my mind, but something—maybe whatever that guy injected me with earlier—holds me back.

●

**A SOLEMN HUM** comes up from the remaining crowd, and I realize how substantially thinned our numbers are.

At least half of Dodge City has Sacrificed itself.

When the snakes are reduced to a couple of gorged blobs, Dalton raises his hands to halt the hum, adjusting his mask to wipe sweat from his nose. "Today is a day that will live forever in ... " He cuts himself short with a cackle. "Who am I kidding? Harry Crews wants you to drink until you vomit bile and shards of liver, then beat the Immortal Souls out of one another!"

He produces the Harry Crews Effigy, already burning, and holds it over the Sacrifice Pit to illuminate what has been accomplished there. When it crumbles, he lets it go and holds up his burned hands for all to see, the effigy's condom hanging from his wrist.

●

**WHAT TO DO** with the Sacrificed Bodies?

I see the Proprietor of the Suicide Cemetery surveying the pit. Soon Dalton appears, still masked, to confront him. The Police, wary of confrontation on this holy day, watch from the peripheries.

**I GO** to the Bar, where a lot of people are already gathered, and crane to see the TV, streaming live from the pit.

"These are not Suicides," the Proprietor of the Suicide Cemetery, who I can tell isn't long for this Town, is saying. "They were murdered by the spirit of Harry Crews. Helpless as lemmings. What I'm interested in, Suicide-wise, is volition. The desire to cross over, sight unseen. To go from somewhere to nowhere, not from somewhere to a more vivid somewhere, as those who Sacrifice themselves inevitably believe they are doing. I'm interested in those who cross over with no beckoning hand on the other side."

Growls in the Bar, breaking glass.

Dalton turns confidently toward the camera to say, "But, you have to understand, the Death of Harry Crews has pulled our whole substructure out from under us. He was our bedrock. A Town without a Patron Saint is a, well … Let me just say that the sanctification of burial in the Suicide Cemetery is the only order left for those of us who gave their lives today. Surely, you can't claim that denying them … "

"*Gave* their lives?" the Proprietor almost chokes. "What kind of Suicide *gives* life? No, sir. Suicide is about *wasting* life, not giving it. This isn't what I came to Dodge City to be a part of. Not at all. Unless … " His eyes light up here. "Unless you might be willing to consider a compromise."

Dalton removes his mask to make an expression of possible willingness.

"Harry Crews," the Proprietor says. "Harry Crews, himself. Bring me him as a Suicide, for the Plot of Honor, and I'll take all the others with him. As Handmaidens."

Dalton blanches at the blasphemy, perhaps affectedly for the camera, though I doubt it. "Harry Crews is *not* a Suicide!" he bellows. "Death is the explanation for the Death of Harry Crews! He was better than the best of us. I'm talking about peace for The Dodge City Dead, not an abomination of the order of … "

"But surely," the Proprietor interrupts, with a grin like he's enjoying twisting The Dodge City Logic against itself, "you're not accusing Harry Crews of being *acted upon*, of falling out of his own Will and pitifully into the hands of simple Death, are you?"

Dalton puts the mask back on.

●

**I MUSCLE** my way out of the Bar before seeing how this all ends.

# Beasts in a Prayer Meadow and
# a Litany of Alterna-Faulkners

**P**AST THE SACRIFICE PIT where the glutted snakes are sleeping, I make my way to the Suicide Cemetery on foot. I want to see it before the Harry Crews controversy paves it over. Also, I want to clear my mind, bring myself back down to earth in the way that only a solitary walk along its surface can.

I can feel The Dodge City Folklore shifting and cracking open in the wake of its Patron Saint's passing, just as I felt the substructures of my former life cracking when I first heard Dalton's speech upon arriving here.

I take comfort in the pattern, though I don't try to tease out what it portends.

●

**THE WALK** to the Suicide Cemetery is longer than it looked from my window.

After a slow hike through waving grass, I find myself in a clearing defined by rock piles. They're too far away to make out in detail, and look fairly crude, but I can tell they're man-made, monuments or markers held over from The Pagan Dodge City, back before we'd known that Dodge City was its own Pagan Analogue. In other words, as far as I understand, these things have been here all along.

It's lighter here than it was in Town, like I've walked all night into the dawn.

Now I see others, heads wrapped in shrouds and faces down, hugging themselves tightly around the bottoms of their ribs, walking in loose, private circles.

They surround a center defined by two large creatures, similar to one another but not of the same species. Both resemble giant horses, between thirty and forty feet tall and eighty or ninety long. One has tusks, like an estranged relative of the mastodon, while the other's head is lost in a mane long and full as a weeping willow, hanging to the ground.

As the shrouded and murmuring faithful trace their wide arcs around this center (remaining always between the creatures and the rock piles, beyond which lies naked steppe), the creatures brush up against one another, stare into each other's eyes, and then retreat, an air of sadness hovering hugely between them.

It occurs to me, as I stand at a safe distance, that they are ruminating on the impossibility of interbreeding. I can tell this with a certainty that reveals a change in state I hadn't, until now, perceived in myself. Like two mules of different provenances, the species-pull between them is great, but not as great as the reality that there is nowhere left for it to go. They paw the ground, sniffing and snorting, and then turn, lumber away, and then repeat.

The faithful continue their prayer-loops, mouths working constantly on syllables that hover well beneath the semantic sphere.

●

**I BREATHE OUT**, and out, and out, spitting out my mind until it's empty.

Then I fall in step, tracing this same circle around the beasts, aware suddenly (and utterly, as if I'd always been aware) that this is the antechamber to the Suicide Cemetery, invisible from my Room's window.

Into me come fresh syllables, a mantra I didn't know I had. I open my mouth and give voice to a litany of Faulkners:

"The Greek Faulkner. The Faulkner who wrote a 10,000-page novel and nothing else. The Yankee Faulkner. The Lady

Faulkner. The Faulkner still to come. The Faulkner who re-
nounced Faulkner to become Dante. The Hebrew Faulkner.
The Faulkner who sold his name to a cabal of others. The
Faulkner who ate his children to become a Folk God Faulkner. The Faulkner who refused his calling and campaigned for
a new one. The Faulkner who wrote *Buddenbrooks* at nineteen
and died of typhoid in Africa at twenty-one. The reanimated
Faulkner, walking among us. The Chinese Faulkner. The Ouli-
po Faulkner. The Faulkner who never heard about Death. The
Faulkner who didn't put too fine a point on the mysteries of
race. The fossil Faulkner, whose bones were read and tran-
scribed by German archeologists at Knossos, who then, based
on what they'd learned, produced *The Complete Works of Faulkner*. The Faulkner whose works were melted down to fill a
coin-operated puppet. The Twitter-quip Faulkner. The Faulkner who wrote one word per day and one word per book. The
Millennial-curse Faulkner, whose pages are used to blot the
deadly sores they engender. The cold, cold reptile Faulkner.
The paid-by-the-word Faulkner who never cashed his checks
because he couldn't find time. The Faulkner who wrote for
God alone (and who God alone has read). The disembodied
Faulkner, whispering up from a pit. The joke Faulkner, trotted
out for kids at county fairs. The pure-math Faulkner, conjured
only by rare and fearsome derivatives. The revenant Faulkner,
shut away in the attic of a condemned mansion, pushing hand-
written scraps under the door for a slavering half-wit Keeper to
gather up and bear away to Harvard."

This is my mantra, I think, proud to have something that's
truly mine.

But as I watch all the others, heads shrouded, murmuring as
they circle the infertile beasts, I wonder, unhappily: What if it's
their mantra, too?

# *A Hasty Verschönerung*

**T**IME GETS SLOW in the Prayer Meadow as I trudge with the shrouded figures, worrying about uniqueness and my place in the world.

I fall into a waking sleepwalk, my eyes milked-over such that I'm trying to discern my thoughts etched onto what looks like a candlelit wall of whitish wax, rising like a cliff out of the waves.

I'm still in this state, deciphering one wax-scratched word at a time, uttering none of them, listening to the frustrated, horsey beasts chew, when the Messenger arrives.

The sleepy Prayer Meadow is thrown into action, fast and shambolic:

In comes Big Pharmakos, decked out in religious garb, genuflecting in a way I read as a signal that he needs to talk to me. I hurry toward him, realizing, with a shiver, that his appearance has likely pulled me back from the brink of losing myself among the unfinished plots of the Suicide Cemetery.

I follow him into a ragged tent-like enclosure, where everyone's whispering, "Inspector … emergency audit … from time to time … never know when … have to cloak … rearrange … retrofit … redact, dissemble … by no means, at any cost … right now, man, today, right this minute … no, here, in Dodge City, a full audit, no stone left … "

●

**THINGS CHANGE** fast. There's no longer any Prayer Meadow, no longer any beasts or celebrants. My Gap outfit is neither warm nor solemn enough for the change in atmosphere.

Big Pharmakos and I stick together as the locales get shuffled and cloaks of all sizes and natures get thrown over all offending aspects of the Town.

"Like when those two Red Cross Inspectors came to Theresienstadt in '44? To see what the Nazis had been up to? And the Nazis mustered all the stick figures they'd been making to clean the place up ... like really clean it up, spotless top to bottom, so when the Swiss dropped in, it'd all look aboveboard, like some kind of summer camp."

My lips feel pasted-on, so I leave off trying to reply.

"They called it the Great Verschönerung," Big Pharmakos continues. We are, as far as I can tell, no longer in a space of any kind. "Really cleaned the fuck out of what, until the moment the Swiss got there, would have looked pretty doubtlessly to you or I like the home of some genuine badness. And at least the Nazis had some forewarning—look around you; we're doing this all on the fly, our pants down and tripping us up."

Slices of Dodge City filter by, blurring as expert stagehands shuffle them into hiding.

I chew my tongue until Big Pharmakos stuffs a wooden spoon in my direction, which I begin to chew instead, though it's far less satisfying.

**"THERE SHE IS!"** shouts Big Pharmakos later on, as we're standing in a windy parking lot with 7-11 soda cups and hubcaps whipping our shins, a smell of gas and fur in the air.

I look, and see a very tall, androgynous figure, in a smart pantsuit and high heels, carrying a bundle wrapped in sheets. The bundle is about twice the size of a baby.

A pizza box smacks the back of my head, and I see the air fill with dandruff and crumbs.

●

**WHEN I REGAIN** my composure, I see the double-baby-sized bundle reach out a hand and unravel just enough of the cloth she's wrapped in to peek out. I can see her eyes, looking hard at the Town, taking it all in. She's an exact scale replica of her Handler, who I sense is both her mother and her father.

Big Pharmakos crouches behind an old Ford Galaxie on cinder blocks and tugs at my Gap pants to get me to do the same. "Stay out of sight, man, seriously!" he barks.

Thus crouched, we watch as the Inspector appraises us through her wrapped bundle. She whispers to her Handler, who makes notes on a black device.

The longer we remain crouched here, the more I feel my usual subjective orientation slipping out of its grooves. Ever since Industry Ed swapped me out, it's been hard to remain in my body.

●

**THE INSPECTOR'S** perspective subsumes me:

The cloth I'm wrapped in smells like Irish Spring laundry detergent. I like how tightly it contains me. I feel swaddled and safe. When I whisper, my Handler carries me to the next site. I stare through the gap in the cloth over my eyes, taking in all I can of this Town, trying to see it for what it is.

I know this feeling. It's the feeling I get in a dream when the dreamworld has something in its heart that it doesn't want me to see.

It deflects and distracts me, bounces me off its surfaces, tempts me with falsehood. The air itself tells me that what I'm looking for must be here, but it will not let me find it.

I grow angry in my bundle. I squirm in my Handler's hands. This isn't good. The people of this Town are hiding something, and it's my job to find out what.

**AFTER THE MANIA** of cloaking Dodge City dies down, it's like there's been a tornado. Telephone poles are split and wires are sparking; dogs lay spread out in the street; hydrants bubble dejectedly; mushrooms sprout in puddles.

Big Pharmakos and I walk out of this parking lot and around a corner in a worn-out city that might as well be Detroit. People who seem to have nothing to do with our lives hustle us on the street.

Finally, we see a Cracker Barrel lit up at the end of the block, and hurry toward it, hands in our pockets, shouldering off the advances of five or six people between here and there.

●

**INSIDE**, we brood over coffee and burgers and partially frozen fries. I play with the wooden spoon that Big Pharmakos gave me, admiring the tooth marks I put in it.

Aside from a waitress, there's no one here except Gottfried Benn, hunched and alone a few tables over. I instinctively feel my wallet for $60 and find I don't have it.

Not now, I think, but he's already on his way over to our booth.

"Heard about the Inspector?" Big Pharmakos asks him.

Gottfried Benn shrugs, as if, as far as he's concerned, he's still in the Diner he usually haunts.

Realizing that he wants his $60, Big Pharmakos sighs and says, "We don't have any cash right now. Order whatever you want and give me the bill. I'll put it on my card."

After he's ordered, Big Pharmakos says, "The thing that sells this restaurant as truly being what it claims to be is not the kitsch in the gift shop but the waitstaff in the dining room," abridging what I assume is a joke classic among comedians of his generation.

Gottfried Benn, surprising us both, laughs hysterically.

I look out the window at giant piles of scrap metal and rolls of wire and tubing as they tremble in the atmosphere, on the verge of resolving into robots.

None of us has anything to do aside from slouching away from ourselves, trying to become anonymous in the service of keeping Dodge City plausible as Not-Dodge-City until the Inspector leaves without finding what she's looking for.

Not that I have any guess as to what this might be, and of course, I can't ask around since everyone's busy pretending it doesn't exist. So I make my best effort at ceasing to be myself, in case, latent within me, lies the clue.

●

**WHEN THE BILL ARRIVES**, Big Pharmakos pays for everything, and we go back to the halfway house where we're registered under false names. The People of Dodge City have fled their normal dwellings, like after a hurricane, and are living in halfway houses, detention centers, refugee camps, ghettos, and, a lucky few, at the Cottonwood Suites on the corner of E. 39th and SE. Huron.

There are even some former Dodge City residents dressed as assault-rifle-wielding FEMA troops, ushering everyone else around, keeping certain people behind fences and giving others emergency medical care.

At the halfway house, Big Pharmakos and I sit on plastic chairs with wool hats pulled low over our eyes, holding out our forearms to watch our Danzig tattoos fade with age.

●

**IN THE ABANDONED DODGE CITY**, which exists in the same space but not in the same state as this hastily assembled

Detroit, I, as the Inspector, ride one of those two beasts from the Prayer Meadow, while my Handler rides the other.

We stampede up and down the empty streets, knocking down storefronts and ripping up pavement. We've ripped out the beasts' eyes and are steering them with our hands shoved deep into the sockets, massaging their brains, enjoying ourselves despite the seriousness of our task.

The harder we massage, the faster and more triumphantly the beasts run. My Handler is big, sitting high on her beast's back, her hands shoved into the sockets up to the elbows, probably meeting in the middle, but I'm a tiny bundle, still wrapped in sheets, stuck onto my beast like a wooly mothball entangled in its mane.

●

**THIS IS ALMOST** all there is to the vision. But I see one other thing:

A dark space, like a small room, basically a closet. Its boundaries are indistinct, and there's no apparent door, but it's definitely enclosed because the thing inside is raging to get out.

It slams against its imprisonment, sweating and spitting, eyes and nose watering with fury. It roars, tearing indiscriminately at itself and its surroundings.

As it struggles, my vision segues away from the Inspector, who's leaning in to the hole in her beast's head, whispering. The more she whispers, the louder the beast bellows, growing cacophonous, like she's blowing into a hunting horn.

The clouds thicken, and the thing in that cramped space rages all the harder against the entropy holding it back from heeding this call. It is drawn to the Inspector from the centermost inside point of Dodge City; this much is clear. What it wants to do to the Inspector, or what the Inspector wants to do to it, is not.

"Dude," I say, trying to keep my voice down, in Big Pharmakos' direction, "that thing is about to get out. I think it's what the Inspector is looking for."

But in the plastic chair beside me, instead of Big Pharmakos, sits a skinny shirtless guy with *Rain Dogs* tattooed across his chest and a belt around his left arm. He slumps to the ground when I get up to leave.

I run into the semi-present street scene, my accelerating footsteps falling into rhythm with the hoofbeats and the bellowing of those brain-driven beasts, until we're running as one, toward or away from that confined furious thing in the dark, about to break free as the whole night sky lights up red with the Inspector's call.

# *Another Sacrifice*

**W**HEN THAT FURIOUS BEING breaks loose, all of Dodge-City-as-Detroit goes into a panic.

Except, it's surprising:

The being, which had seemed titanic, even potentially world-destroying in my vision, turns out, in its current exposed form, to be tiny and pitiful. Like the outside air has sucked the life out of it.

We all stop where we are as the Inspector and her Handler dismount from their beasts and stand before the thing they've summoned.

We make a circle in the Town Square, closing in around the worldly manifestation of that titanic thing, which now appears hardly bigger than a baby, wrapped in the same linens and rags as the Inspector, herself. It clears a rag-strip from its eyes and surveys the circular crowd closing in, then pulls the linen back in place.

It appears the Inspector has succeeded in summoning forth the Living Heart of Dodge City—that which we tried so hard to conceal—except, in so doing, she's remade it in her own image.

The force of this revelation seems temporarily to deactivate the actual Inspector, who hangs slack near the circle's edge, graciously or impotently affording us time to think.

●

WE CALL a quorum in the back room of the Bar, among bags of empty cans and decommissioned arcade games and gambling consoles. There are some folding chairs, which we unfold in order to sit in a circle like people thinking rationally about what to do.

There isn't, though you'd think for sure there would be, any real sense of hurry. It feels as though the worst has already happened, and now all we have to do is react.

Once we've taken our time, our thinking amounts to: 'We could Sacrifice this pseudo-Inspector to expiate two scandals at once. First, to return our Town to Dodge City and purge it of whatever veneer of Detroit it's accrued and, second, to send the real Inspector on her way, without having found what she came here for.'

The deeper and less palatable notion that, in so doing, we'll be Sacrificing the Living Heart of Dodge City, itself, goes unmentioned, though I doubt I'm the only one considering it.

In any case, as we have so often before, we agree that Sacrifice is the appropriate response to the turn our lives have taken.

●

**WE PROCESS** out of the Bar and back into the ravening crowd, which has surrounded the baby-Inspector-to-be-Sacrificed, as well as the real Inspector and her Handler, hands slick in gloves of brain Blood. Their beasts lay Dead beside them, their race run.

Professor Dalton is called out of whatever fearsome reclusion he's descended into. Quickly outfitting his Mobile Sacrifice Station, he rolls into the circle where the ritual is to take place, donning the familiar golden-beaked bird mask.

Big Pharmakos has agreed to serve as Executioner. He shows up dressed in a green, pink, and yellow jester outfit.

"It is said," he explains, "that in Medieval Spain, or Germany, the Town Executioner would always dress in the brightest and most garish possible colors, so both townsfolk and strangers alike could distinguish him at a glance, and keep well clear until their, heh heh, number was called."

"Who says that?" I ask.

"The Jester Costume package." His voice jumps an octave as he zips the back of his suit.

"You mean the Executioner Costume package?"

But he's already put on the cap, and bells are ringing in his ears.

●

**SCANNING THE CROWD**, we see everyone spread out on picnic blankets like spectators at the Civil War, eating sandwiches and drinking wine.

The baby-Inspector, docile inside its linens, is brought forth as Big Pharmakos lurks in the background, sharpening his knife.

Dalton preaches about the Beheading of Saint John the Baptist, the Sacrifice he's decided to base today's on. "Herod wanted to marry Herodias, the wife of his own brother. But the Gospels are clear: there can be only one brother per bed."

The crowd makes chewing sounds. I'm seated on the platform but off to one side, in a spectatorial rather than an instrumental position.

"Except for the prophet, there are only enemy brothers and mimetic twins in the text."

A sign-language Interpreter stands beside Dalton, hurrying to keep up, while Big Pharmakos, in full regalia, looms behind them, sharpened knife by his side.

Dalton pauses to wonder aloud about whether what he wants to say next is from Wittgenstein's reading of Hegel or Bernhard's reading of Wittgenstein.

The crowd grows restless. "Move it along, Professor!" someone shouts, and a cheer goes up. Big Pharmakos raises his knife and the cheer magnifies.

"To Herodias then," Dalton blurts, "to Saint John the Baptist! To the eternal war between desire and truth, mimicry and representation, brother and wife and brother-wife and the knife … self-love and other-love and love-love and Bloodlust!"

●

**FESTIVE BEFORE**, the crowd is now approaching Argentine soccer game mania. They've been drinking and gorging on meat and sugar, so by now they're well beyond the ideal state of readiness to witness the bloody demise they've been promised.

Now they're charging the stage, throwing cans and knocking out teeth.

We were planning to drop a mirror over the actual beheading so the crowd could see the pitiless desire in their own eyes while knowing that the moment of sanctified violence was transpiring just behind what they could see, namely their own eyes reflected ad infinitum, which would in turn be … Anyway, now it's a pyramid of broken glass.

There's shrieking and Big Pharmakos is slashing at random with his big knife, the bells in his Jester cap ringing off the hook, and there's biting, and some people have knives of their own out, and others have firecrackers, and others, naturally, have guns, so now everything's on fire and I've almost been shot twice.

Dalton, meanwhile, is praying aloud to Sade and Pasolini and Burroughs and Genet, on the ground, kicking his feet in the air, begging Harry Crews, wherever and whatever he is now, to look upon us with favor and understanding.

**WHEN IT'S OVER**, the Dead cover the entirety of what's now known as Sacrifice Square, and Detroit has indeed been expiated, the air cleared to reveal Dodge City as if it'd been there all along. It smells like laundry fresh from the dryer.

And the Inspector and her Handler are gone, though an unsettled atmosphere remains, a sense that perhaps they've simply borne their report off to another location and will in time be back. Or that a Higher-Up in whatever Order they belong to will return in their place. The Proprietor of the Suicide Cemetery is gone, as well, shoved down into history, already part of a more primitive era, one in which we deserved his expertise more than we do now.

I walk down a side street, zipping the windbreaker I find myself wearing while trying to remember what happens at the end of *The Wizard of Oz* and whether all this is like that or not really.

# PHASE IV:

## *A Hard Winter*

# *Our Christmas Bullheads Speak* Molloy

**S**HORT, shortening afternoons into December. I'm in my Room, hanging out with Big Pharmakos, who's in a comedy rut. "The worst is when my jokes for the year run out before the year does," he says, looking crushed when I don't laugh.

We listen to Scott Walker's *Bish Bosh* without comment. The record plays on and on, and we're never quite sure when it's repeating. I ruminate on my role in the Town's salvation from the Inspector, wondering how willingly I accepted it vs. whether it was foisted upon me, and if so, by whom? Why wasn't I indifferent, planning, as I still am, to move on as soon as my modest savings run out?

Following the old Dodge City saying whereby a man is said to have said, "I've brought my lawn chair in off the lawn so that my pregnant wife might have someplace indoors to sit," Big Pharmakos brings in a lawn chair from the alley behind the Hotel and sits on it rubbing his belly and watching the phone.

As soon as I see him on the chair, I can't remember where he was sitting before.

When the phone rings, he puts it on speaker, pulling me out of my thoughts. It's our Benefactor, who only calls at this time of year. With no small amount of menace, she says, "I'm gonna get you all something nice for Christmas. To recover from the shock you've sustained."

She goes on to explain that everyone will be given a Bullhead that speaks lines from Beckett's *Molloy*, a lucky charm against the Evil Spirits loosed by the loss of Harry Crews and the subsequent trauma of the Inspector's visit. "These are uncertain times," she concludes, "but there is no uncertainty about *Molloy*."

We will each get a Bullhead, she continues, impregnated with a section of the text. We are to keep it in a cardboard box rather than mounting it on the wall like a trophy, and kneel to kiss it gently each time we pass by, throughout the winter. Following this, it will bullishly speak a line or two before falling silent like the severed head it is.

"The Slaughtering of the Bulls is underway," she concludes. "Why don't you turn on your TV?"

●

**IN THE SLAUGHTERHOUSE**, all is industry. The Slaughterers are arranged vertically, according to shifts. Some are resting against the ceiling, tied tight in harnesses, huffing meth from open vents. Those who are ready to step to the slaughter have been winched to ground level and are donning their rubber smocks, sharpening their blades, which, in honor of *Molloy*, are fashioned to resemble the Malaysian Kris, one of Beckett's favorite weapons.

Those by the ceiling huff their meth and dance against their restraints, feeling the energy for a twenty-one-hour slaughter shift shoot through their necks to their hearts. They have to work triple shifts this year due to layoffs, while all the laid-off workers stand just outside, stone cold sober, hoping against hope in laughable vain to be rehired.

On the kill floor, along with the winching and the Kris-sharpening, are the machinations of the High Priests, all dressed like Dalton, mimicking his mannerisms. They wander among the fatted bulls holding open their Everyman Editions of Beckett's *Trilogy*, whispering down the rows of ears, massaging them with their tongues while painlessly imparting sentences like bacon-wrapped pills.

The Slaughterers follow behind the High Priests with their Krisses ready to hack through muscle, sinew, and bone once the words have found purchase in the Bullheads, hacking off said heads at precisely the right moment to seal those words into undying instinct, bypassing all cortices to bore into the stratum of the biological-inevitable, as deep a drive as that of putrefaction.

●

**THIS IS HOW** it should happen, one head at a time, until there are enough for all of us.

But, as if it weren't obvious, a disclaimer flashes across the TV screen: "Now things are going wrong."

Big Pharmakos turns up the volume while I turn down the Scott Walker.

It goes wrong when the Slaughterers lose control of their weapons, and no one can get through to the High Priests, who are still whispering dervishlike into the Bulls' spooked ears. The Bulls seem to have been emotionally prepared for slaughter, but now they can tell that something worse is underway.

The Rope Operators, themselves spooked, winch down the last of the next shift of Slaughterers, and the meth-vents, unmouthed, are left open to the whole of the interior, fogging the place so thick that Big Pharmakos and I think it's a tracking problem on our TV. We wipe at the screen, to no avail.

The Slaughterers, all of them on the kill floor now, are hacking and sawing hard at the Bulls' necks, sharing weapons, while the High Priests, their own glands swollen with meth now, read on and on in *Molloy*, fingers sweating through the pages.

Nothing's happening to the Bulls, by which I mean none of them are turning headless.

They are, rather, it seems, banding together. The Slaughterers saw harder than ever, while, in between waves of static, we see the many bulls becoming several, growing at first proportionately, and then disproportionately, larger. Soon they're as large as those beasts from the Prayer Meadow. Ropes whip all up and down the Slaughterhouse, tangling in the horns of Bulls that are now ...

One Bull.

One giant Bull, its neck sawed-at and distressed but far from severed, shooting upward like a jack-in-the-box toward the roof.

It breathes the meth deep with eyes awakening to a new kind of life, while the High Priests cling to its ears and continue to whisper Beckett like that's all they know how to do. The Slaughterers are now far below, hacking comically at its ankles, barely breaking skin.

●

**THE SLAUGHTERHOUSE ROOF** comes off. The Bull now stands towering over the unemployment line outside. Many of the High Priests have fallen off, but some remain, entwined in the rigging that clings to the Bull's enraged and stretched-thin hide. Some of them are even perched inside the Bull's ears like ticks.

They whisper on and on, and then the Bull, meth steaming from its nostrils, begins to speak: "Unfortunately, I do not quite know what floor I am on; perhaps I am only on the mezzanine," it says, into the open air, like it's thinking up Beckett's words for the first time ever. "I have lost my stick. That is the outstanding event of the day, for it is day again. Sine qua non, Archimedes was right."

For a moment, none of us knows what's happening. What's really happening, I mean, above and beyond what's obviously happening.

Then, all at once, our phones ring. It's our Benefactor, speaking in a rage such as we've never heard before: "It's left *Molloy* and gone on to *Malone Dies!* Kill the High Priests! If this Bull is allowed to reach *The Unnamable*, Dodge City is finished!"

# The Year in Evil

**I**T DOESN'T take long for our Benefactor to order Professor Dalton to appear on her behalf.

When we see him standing on the same platform we used to Sacrifice the Inspector's proxy, Big Pharmakos and I leave my Room and filter into Sacrifice Square along with the rest of Dodge City.

By the time we get out there, Dalton's presenting our Benefactor's idea:

There is to be a second amalgamation, by the logic that one of something calls for another.

After flattening thirty houses, the Bull has huddled in a pit in the very Center of Town. I understand this to be a reamed-out version of the enclosed space the Inspector's proxy emerged from, as if that void, once opened, can never close.

It's down in there now, becalmed but still profoundly frightening, lowing up lines like, "That's it, reminisce. Here and there, in the bed of a crater, the shadow of a withered lichen. And nights of three hundred hours. Dearest of lights, wan, pitted, least fatuous of lights."

We try to close our ears to this, so as to open them to our Benefactor's instructions on the amalgamation that's to occur, which will constitute this year's Year in Evil event and, I suppose, replace our Christmas presents.

"Normally," Big Pharmakos explains in a whisper, "we gather up all the Evil that's transpired in the country, and in the world, that year—all the insensate Death by metal and gas, temperature and bone—and make it as if it all occurred right here, in downtown Dodge City, in the span of the week leading up to today in a hellish spree whose enormity reality groans to accommodate. It's really more of a New Year's thing, but desperate times and all ...

"By setting it all here, we spare the rest of the country, and world, the misery of its having happened there. This, we feel, is the least we can do as citizens of a larger scheme, since the Evil at the Heart of Dodge City is already infinite—whereas, in other Towns, a little less makes a big difference."

●

**NORMALLY**, a Demon is chosen: one Dodge City citizen, man or woman, appears before us shrouded in black muslin, wrapped in thick, punishing rope.

Professor Dalton condemns this wrapped figure for all the Evil it perpetrated this year, beyond all reason and comprehension, beyond even the defining edges of lurid fantasy, far out though they be, and growing ever further, like the expanding universe, itself. Then he condemns it to walk, on and on, into the steppe where it will never see another living soul. Whether finally it will emerge among its own kind, on the Plane of Evil, or wander forever unaccompanied on this one, where Evil visits, and rents, but does not yet reside, is not for any of us to say.

●

**THE BOUND FIGURE** appears before us now. "But this year," Dalton explains, "something else is to befall the Demon. Something that may save us yet."

*What?* we all wonder.

Then we see: the Demon is to be served up to the Bull as an offering and morsel, to plug its *Malone*-muttering mouth.

The Slaughterers remove the winch from the Slaughterhouse and hook the bound Demon onto it. Then they winch it into the air, where it dangles for all to see, before they lower it into the Bull's pit.

When it hits bottom, tipping off its feet to lie on its side, we all stand back in anticipation, waiting to see how the Bull will consume it.

"Choke! Choke!" we chant at the Bull, desperate for its speech to cease.

But the Bull only looks up at us, winks, and resumes speaking *Malone Dies*, working steadily toward *The Unnamable* like a child reciting the alphabet.

The High Priests clinging to its ears have been crushed against the edges of the pit, impacted straight into the fossil record. We can smell the Slaughterhouse smoke in the air, hardening into a cloud that will hover over us for months to come.

Then, our pulses quickening to the point where we fear losing consciousness, we see the Bull wink again, and lean in, beginning to whisper into the Demon's muslin shroud, its tremendous tongue against its new companion's Evil Head.

The gesture is motherly, protective, perhaps flirtatious. The awful voice stops, and in this way we are saved, but afflicted by a sudden jealousy, desperate to hear what we had, a moment ago, been desperate to stop hearing.

The Demon laughs knowingly, like the two of them are now conspiring against us.

At a loss for how to proceed, we go to the Movies to unwind.

# "Would You Like to
# Go Someplace Else?"

**I** **HIT BOTTOM** in the Movie Theater, where *The Wicker Man* plays on endless loop.

After sending up a distress signal from my seat, an employee escorts me into a side area. He hands me a towel, thoughtfully warmed, and a cup of spicy lemon tea.

"I haven't seen you since you were a boy and your father was younger than you are now," he shudders, when I've handed him back the towel. I can tell he's warming up to unload a reverie of comics and baseball cards, bats and mitts, borrowed bikes, working on the hot rod with Uncle Skip on Saturday afternoon, the garage door open to all that fresh pollen, somebody's brother's Telecaster against the back wall, and a litany of what used to cost a dime ...

"Spare me," I groan, putting my foot down, kicking my ankle against the wall to scrape off the maudlin that's started to condense from the air.

He shakes his head at the impudence of youth and rummages in his pocket for what he says are the tears he would like to cry. The tag on the chest of his blue jumpsuit says Little Bird.

"That you?" I ask, nudging the tag to change the subject.

He seems to think I mean him in general, his whole person. He nods in the affirmative.

Then he asks, "Would you like to go someplace else?"

I nod, wondering if I could do worse than here.

He nods again, and we set off down a hall, doors with name-tags lining our way. The offices of the Theater's Management give way slowly to those of the key players in The Dodge City Film Industry.

"How far would you like to go?" he asks.

"Keep going," I say.

●

**"NICE HALL**, eh?" he pipes up, a few hours later.

After a few more hours, we come to an end.

"Okay," he pats my elbow. "There you are. More lemon tea? More warm towel?"

I decline, and he's gone.

Beyond the door is an interval of climbing. Up I go, through a hot, dusty afternoon, not quite hand-over-hand but my feet have to wedge in at diagonals to retain purchase. At first it's thrilling, then I get to wishing it were over. It's too far, too high; I don't like it anymore.

I can tell it's somewhere in Southeast Asia, Thailand or Vietnam, and that I won't get to stop climbing until I reach China. I can see it way overhead, higher than I've ever climbed before.

●

**AFTER WHAT FEELS LIKE YEARS**, I arrive in China. I have a thick beard now, a new accent, and something wrong with my back.

A medicine man at the top heals me in a green meadow.

Families picnic all around me; children chase balls through grass and air. Kites tangle, beget new kites.

I am fantastically hungry. Carts are set up on all the margins, grilling meat and dough, ladling out juices from a plastic vat. I want to buy as much as whatever currency I find in my pockets will let me, but I find none there.

I lose the afternoon in worry.

The picnics abate, remembered in monuments of plastic wrap and beer bottles.

Alone in the evening, I spy, just down the hillside, a gas station with a convenience store. It seems to have only appeared after it got dark. Maybe I can borrow or steal some food there, or find a few coins along the way.

As I set out toward it, some older men dressed in robes appear, whispering behind and beside me.

"You shall find that difficult," says one, after much conference with the others. "You shall not reach that place."

●

**AND IT'S TRUE**. I've been walking at least an hour and am no nearer than when I started. It has, however, gotten darker, as though I've made progress through time but not through space, just as I could have without moving at all.

As it gets darker, the night tends toward red, not black. As it gets redder, these men make themselves comfortable in a place whose contours I can't yet perceive, while more file in, their jocular voices fading as they draw near.

It's now full red. The picnic meadow and gas station spread has been rolled up, replaced by folding chairs under a low ceiling, at the end of a corridor with nooks cut into the wall, faces peering out between shelves of devotional paraphernalia.

I am shown to a seat, as well. A bowl of steaming tea is placed in my hands, and a plate of grilled meat on sticks is laid out on a low table. The man beside me indicates that I should take some.

In front of us, through a pane of tempered glass, is an even redder place, sealed off at all its edges.

There is an audience of fifty or sixty people around me now, all of them riveted on the glass.

From far down the line one whispers something, and I can hear the whisper approaching me, ear to mouth to ear, until the man next to me spits out a mouthful of English: "This is Red Chamber. It is the room where something must happen. For this, we wait."

I ask how long they've all been waiting, entering my whisper back down the line of seated heads, which I term the Translation Centipede.

It comes back, "Thirty thousand years."

## Escape from Red Chamber

**W**E'RE ALL in our seats, staring at the glass.

I snack; they talk.

Just when this all seems poised to go on forever, a gas begins to flow, frosting the pane before our eyes.

It's too thick and hazy to tell who's who, or what's what, but there's one humanoid figure inside and one less so, and they're going at it hard.

There's slamming against the glass, which clears away the condensation for a moment, affording a temporary window.

It's paw and pod, finger and fang, tail and tentacle, limbs of numerous sorts intertwining and going for the kill.

The human looks like a guy about my age, in a sweaty T-shirt and jeans, and the thing that's killing him, or that he's killing, looks like a mound of Flesh that nature was unable to devise an animal form for.

The audience sits quietly, politely, watching, and watching me watch, as if waiting to read something on my face that will help them grasp the significance of the spectacle. Maybe this is their reason for bringing me here and feeding me dinner.

After some parts that are so gruesome I have to look away, the guy I resemble stands there panting, the thing slain beside him.

It's unclear what role the gas played in this surprising victory, but I feel a tremor of empathetic elation. At the same time, I can't help feeling that it wasn't a fair fight, like the beast in the end served no purpose other than to introduce this new guy, and show what powers he has.

The men look over and see this empathy spread across me, whisper about it to one another. Perhaps they'd hoped I'd be more impressed.

It's quiet for a while, the guy in there pacing, looking out, though I can't tell if he can see us.

Then everyone in the audience turns toward me. The one nearest me whispers, "What're you waiting for?"

I look all around, trying to find something pending to point to.

They shake their heads. The Translation Centipede whirs to life, producing the words, "When, at last, Travelers recover themselves on the other side of the glass, they must go and rejoin themselves there. That is how our Civilization has prospered until today."

They seem disturbed by having to tell me this. I think, Here's my chance! Though I can't tell for what.

"Why aren't you going? Look!" the Centipede says, pointing at the guy inside the glass. "That's you!" it continues, pointing again. "That's you in there! In Red Chamber!"

I look.

"Why are you clogging Red Chamber?" it whispers in my ear. I can feel the gray of its tongue. The guy in there scratches his ear, like he can feel it, too. "What business do you have here? We are waiting, humbly, through the generations, for an infinitesimal taste of the Sublime. Not for you, sweaty and covered in beast Blood."

The guy in there holds his shirt away from himself and checks it out, like he didn't know how stained it was.

I can sense that they want me to go, but I don't yet know how. So I hesitate, and see the guy in there hesitating, too.

"Don't make us do something we've never done before," the Centipede says.

"You want me to be him?" I ask.

The question doesn't compute. "Who are you dividing? There is only one."

I have from time to time consented to say, "That's mine," regarding something that isn't really mine, to avoid a worse alternative, but I've never before consented to say, "That's me," when I was equally uncertain. But today I cross a new line. "Thanks for the hospitality," I say, getting ready for the gas.

**NOW I'M THE GUY** in there, which is to say I'm the guy in here, on my way out.

Beyond Red Chamber is a network of tunnels, some extremely narrow and others so wide I can't see their edges. At first this seems like a design flaw, but then I remember the steep climb I made to get up here, and am grateful that the descent is more gradual.

As the days start to fall into this new stack, I miss my old self, whoever I used to think I was, surely gone now for good.

I imagine appearing before a first-grade class when I get back, telling them about what I've done. I take the floor, with my anecdotes and briefcase full of examples, after an introduction from their teacher that goes something like, "Here, children, is a man who was changed utterly by his time overseas."

# *A Burnt House*

**I**T'S A FINE, spring-like winter's day in Dodge City as I emerge from the tunnels, my mind full of the wrappers of spent thoughts, and my lungs full of gas.

The journey has left me with the image of a house on a leafy street. Perhaps it's the house I grew up in long before I came to Dodge City, or the one I suppose I'd have to move into if I decided to stay here longterm.

In either case, I search for it now. Squinting through the sun, hearing birds, the ground clean-smelling with snowmelt, I walk across Town. It's the kind of day someone in Prison might imagine as the day of his release, or escape, the day he finally breaks through, from the Inside back to the street where he lives, blinded by the light, free at last, etc.

It's like that scene in one of the *Robin Hood* movies, or several of them, where he comes off the ship and kneels on his Home Shore and starts kissing and then almost eating the sand. It's a less hysterical version of that, occurring, as it is, later in history.

Now I'm on the street I pictured, or one sufficiently like it. No one seems to be around, not even any dogs or parked cars. I want to sit on my porch and get my bearings.

But when I get there, the worst has come to pass:

My house has burned down.

My whole life's worth of rigorously quieted worries about having left the stove on has come to naught, I think, or perhaps to fruition.

The strange thing is that it looks like it's burned down very recently—is even still smoldering in places—but there's no one around. No fire trucks, no onlookers. I wonder if they haven't come yet, or if they've already come and gone, or if they aren't coming, either because they don't know or because they do know, but this knowledge doesn't do anything for them anymore.

I go up to it. A crow comes down from a telephone wire to dance in the ashes, clacking its beak at me. I kick it away before I get any more worked up. As soon as it's gone, I wonder whether it was really there or if my anxiety hatched it. I wish it would come back and reassure me.

But it's just me, trudging among the ashes, looking at what used to be my house (My very first house, I think, on the verge of tears.). Then the tears really come, my first good cry since I left the home I grew up in and took to the road.

My life in Dodge City is over, I think, howling, pitching forward and back, heaving with the tragedy of it. My sneakers burn in the smoldering ash, and I'm on my back stomping my feet and pounding my fists when something catches my eye.

I have to rub it several times before I can get it dry enough to use, but when I do I see my house standing next door, unscathed. Even its lawn looks pretty good.

It takes me a while to realize that this burn site must actually have been my neighbor's house. Kind Old Mr., or Mrs. ... doesn't matter. Mainly I'm elated.

I sit on the curb to collect myself, trying to grasp how I could have made such a fundamental mistake. Finally some cars and pedestrians pass by, like they've been released from a holding pen now that I've come to my senses.

Under my relief, I feel pride. I'm proud of the depth of feeling I was able to muster for my neighbor, my Fellow Man or Woman, the sympathy I felt for their misfortune. That's surely what it was, I decide, not that I ever really thought it was my house that burned.

I mean, they don't even look similar.

●

**WHEN MY BREATHING** and heart rate have stabilized, I stand up, dust the blown ash from my pants and shoes, and go up the driveway of my house. I can see the scorch of my neighbor's backyard, and again a wave of tenderness takes me.

I never carry a key, so I have to force the backdoor open. It's not easy. I have to throw my shoulder and hip into it.

Inside, I take off my shoes, wash my hands and face. Nothing's familiar. Not the soap in the bathroom, not the damp towel, not the waterlogged magazines piled by the toilet. Guess I've been away a long time. Longer than I appreciated, to have forgotten the interior of my own house. I chuckle at what's possible.

I'll make some coffee, I think. Turn on some lights.

It takes me a long while to find where the coffee's kept, the filters. Even working the coffeemaker isn't, dismayingly, buoyed by any force of habit.

I sit at the kitchen table as it's brewing, my mug ready with milk in its bottom. I'll admit that the presence of fresh milk in the fridge doesn't bode well for this house being what I hope it is, given how long I've been away.

I listen to the machine work, and hear footsteps on the stairs, someone coming down, no doubt, to investigate who's here. Just let me have my coffee in peace, I think. Just let me gather the strength to leave, and then I will.

# A Crime in the Steam Room

**W**HOEVER LIVES in this house kindly waits by the stairs until I show myself out. I leave him or her a cup of coffee on the table, putting mine by the sink.

I go back to the Hotel covered in ashes, determined never again to leave my Room.

But it's not ready. I flee the Lobby before they tell who's been staying in it. That's the last thing I need to know. "Tonight," they say. "Tonight at the latest."

●

**I RUN** to the YMCA to decompress in the Steam Room, upstairs from the Spa of the Lamb. But there's no relief here, either. There is, instead, a commotion at the Front Desk.

I slip past with a flash of card, but not without catching parts of the problem: there's been a crime, a murder or a rape, and here are the Police, eager to investigate, but—

The Proprietress, a real Linda Hunt type, won't let them inside with their clothes on. "I'm sorry, folks," she explains, a low wail now issuing through the Steam Room's sealed door, "but rules is rules. My hands are tied on this."

They confer amongst themselves, then come back to the Desk, purchase Guest Passes, receive their towels and combination locks, and file in through the locker room.

●

**DISROBED**, the Police (a coed crew) are in the steam now, as am I and a few old folks and whoever else was in there before, some more visible than others depending on how deep they've gone—the place is known for its corners, some of which go back a long way.

There is a certain encompassing rankness, maybe more than sweat alone would account for, but no definite sign of a body or Blood or any other trappings of what supposedly happened here.

I would say that the Police don't seem particularly concerned about their investigation, but without their uniforms, I can't altogether say which ones the Police are.

Everyone's checking each other out, the thin propriety of these places peeled right away. Some are more feral about it than others, already down on all fours, pulling others down with them.

Things go the way of things, without much prelude, and soon it's a fully-fledged event: arms and legs shoot out from a central mass, breathing through its pores, and there's twisting, grinding, and the grunting of dozens of voices, like a tableau out of Russ Meyer or Ken Russell. When I close my eyes, I picture drumming, midgets, snakes, a fountain spurting red wine.

I'm somewhere in it, buffeted, with one eye out for the body that supposedly set this all in motion.

The Ottoman mosaics that adorn the floors and benches are cracking into sand while the steam apparatus fills the room with boiling water. Scalded hides react with a virulence that feeds the virulence already afoot, turning everyone lobster-red and frantic.

I see how this could go on and on, especially if people don't all come at the same time, which there's no reason to think they will.

●

**THEN** the Police show up.

They're standing in the doorway with Linda Hunt, fully clothed, some with flashlights and some with clipboards.

"Okay folks," they say. "Party's over. We got a call. There's about to be consequences."

The body-mass tries to scatter, but it's stuck tight. Someone's gonna have to do some prying. I wonder if *Unholy Family* has been filming us with a hidden camera.

The Police are stepping among us now, trying to keep their faces from polarizing into disgust and fascination.

●

**WHEN THEY'VE FINISHED** prying everyone apart with olive oil and antihistamines, they line us up for questioning against the wall in the locker room, where the steam goes cold but remains wet.

When it's my turn, a cop with a clipboard takes me aside and asks me to look over what he's written. "Please be gentle but serious with your criticism," he says. "I'm just starting out here, so please try to help me grow."

He looks around to see if anyone else is listening, then continues, "I feel like I have all these ideas, you know; things come to me that seem so cool, so good, and I always think like it'll be so easy to just write them down." He's blushing now. "But then, when I get down to it, just me and the pen and paper, or on my laptop, it all scatters so I can't see it anymore." He catches his breath. "And then it's like I can't focus. I don't know; it's like one minute I have all these ideas and I'm so excited to write, and then the next minute all I want to do is check email and read reviews of movies I'd be better off just watching, given how little work I'm likely to get done."

I keep looking around hoping to discover that he's talking to someone else, but, aside from him, there's no one left but me.

"Anyway," he goes on, "I don't want to just lay this whole trip on you. I mean, I know you have your own shit to worry about and you're probably, I mean ... but, if you'd just read my report here, I'd really appreciate it."

So I read his report. It's mostly standard-issue Police copy, itemizing the crimes that were committed. The only curious thing is that, each time it comes up, instead of "Steam Room," he's written "Peat Bog."

The locker room, as I've already determined, is empty. It's just the two of us and his clipboard. I nod to him encouragingly, but I'm picturing all the others sinking below that Peat Bog, filling with gas and beginning to decompose. "I think this looks good, man. You just have to trust your gut. That's all there is to it, really."

In the course of reading, I've run my wet hands all over the clipboard. Most of the paper has pulped off, so that now I'm wearing a papier-mâché glove on one hand, as is he. Between us, we're wearing most of the report. Just a few strands, right under the clip, remain stuck to the clipboard.

I turn to leave, wondering if I'll be permitted to. As soon as the thought enters my head, I realize how desperate I am to get away from him. I feel the Peat Bog opening underfoot, and have the terrifying sense that he's angling for a way to push me in.

I hurry through the doors, and he doesn't try to stop me.

Outside, the premises are wrapped in CRIME SCENE tape. Crossing the parking lot, I look at my paper-gloved hand, thinking, If Industry Ed could see me now ... without thinking what would happen if he could.

●

# PHASE V:

## *The Dodge City*

## *Folklore*

## *A Trip to the Library*

**B**EYOND EXHAUSTED after the ordeal in the Steam Room, I return to the Hotel, only to learn that my Room still isn't ready. They ask if I'd like another one, but I can't bear the prospect. I tell them I'll be back in a few hours.

In the meantime, I make my way to the Library, determined to dedicate this interval to the lives of others. Unsurprisingly, the thirteen volumes of The Dodge City Folklore take up most of the Library's only shelf. The first ten are *The Complete Works of Harry Crews*, but after these are several volumes of Apocrypha, from which I decide to read a few entries.

# Entry I: The Baby

**A** **MAN** was backing out of a parking lot when he felt his rear tire squish something biological. *Fuck*, he thought, *a cat*. He put his hazard lights on and got out. Expecting to see a tail under his back tire, instead he saw the edges of a diaper and a pool of baby-filling. *Fuck*, he thought, *a baby*.

As he was looking around, trying to determine if getting quickly away was his best move, a woman carrying a bag of groceries appeared behind him, taking in the damage. "Sorry," she said. "I just parked him there for a minute, while I ran in." She indicated the convenience store.

"You parked him in a parking space?"

"Yeah," she replied, eying the meter like perhaps the reason the man was surprised was that her time had expired.

She shrugged, handed him her groceries, and bent down to scoop up the baby-material. Strange but true, it all hung together, even though most of it was liquid. Nothing but a scaly imprint was left on the ground.

She clutched it against her chest as he gave her back her groceries. "Sorry," she repeated, looking at his tire. "It won't happen again."

●

**BUT**, strangely enough, it did. The very next day, in a different part of Town, he backed out over a baby again.

The same woman came out, this time with a pair of boots she'd had resoled, and again gathered up the crushed liquid and said it would never happen again.

It kept happening, day after day, taking on a rhythm. The woman and the man became casual friends, though they could tell it would be wrong to take their relationship further. "It was," he got in the habit of telling whoever would listen, "the only constant in my life during those years."

●

**THIRTY YEARS LATER**, long after that phase of his life had ended, he was shaving at a sink in the YMCA, after a long sit in the Steam Room, when a young man took the sink next to him, laying out his cream and razor. The young man looked at him several times, trying to make sure he really was who he appeared to be.

When the young man was certain, he said, "Sorry to bother you, but I just wanted to say hello. You probably don't remember me, but you used to run me over with your car when I was a baby."

The older man, so lonely for so long, smiled. Shaving cream glopped onto his T-shirt. "Of course I remember you."

The young man smiled, too. "You know, back then, I never understood why my mom kept parking me there, knowing, as she must have, what would happen. But, over the years, it's started to get clearer. To say the least, I see now that it had more to do with her than it ever did with me. That's what I could never accept. I have, over time, learned to stop blaming myself."

The older man waited for the young man to say more, but quickly turned his head away when it appeared that the young man thought he was checking out his abs, which perhaps he was.

Like so, they finished shaving and parted ways.

# Entry II: Diary of a Country Strangler

**T**HEY'D JUST GIVEN BIRTH to their first baby, a beautiful, healthy boy they named Noah, duly blessed, when they decided to move from the capital to a distant, isolated corner of the provinces, hot in summer and cold in winter, where, it was believed, a Letter of Introduction that the husband and father, Jakob, had managed to procure from his advisor in the city, would help him find a job in his field, one that would afford them, at the very least, a means of scraping across the threshold between one day and the next.

So, with this letter in hand, Jakob moved with his wife, Sarah, and the baby, to this distant, shabby Town, like a prelapsarian Dodge City marooned somewhere in the Far Outskirts of the Pale.

Upon arrival, they parceled out their little savings—the dregs of a student stipend, a cashed bond, and the proceeds from the sale of their furniture and a signed Spinoza volume that Sarah had inherited from a now-defunct grandparent years earlier— in order to establish residence in a small, cloudy cottage on the edge of this parochial nowhere where circumstance had forced them to believe their fate lay waiting.

While Sarah came down in her nightclothes before dawn and settled into their one chair in their drafty living room, suckling baby Noah and brushing his several new hairs, Jakob set out for his first day of work.

On his way out, he took up his lunch bag, which contained several scraps of smoked cod, a whole onion which he'd eat like an apple, and two slices of bread, lightly buttered. His gloves (He worked always by hand.) and his mask (sober, form-fitting, burlap) were in a leather sack he kept slung over his shoulder, the same one he'd carried during his student days in the city.

He kissed Sarah and the baby, and departed into the smell of woodfires and the steaming breath of pack animals, stepping gingerly across jagged floes of ice marooned on the dirt road's sidewalks.

●

**IT WAS STILL** before dawn. There would be, he knew, no sleeping in now that his life had begun in earnest. No lazing about and dreaming of the day's openness, of long strolls in sunlight and leisurely cups of coffee and philosophical debate, as there had been in his student days. Even Sarah's signed Spinoza volume, for many years his unwavering companion, was gone, melted down in the furnace of capital.

Walking down that dirt lane, alongside the other working men, both young and old, he thought with a twinge of those bygone days, the feral seriousness they'd had about them that now had come to seem like innocent boys' play: all those belabored, fist-pounding debates of the tangled intersections of the immanent and the transcendent, the coded demonology and eschatology of Isaac Luria and Sabbatai Zevi. This all seemed as harmless now as supping chicken broth through a straw in a paper gown in a hospital bed while very young or very old.

On that first day of his profession, putting such childish things to rest as well as any man could, Jakob strangled three people: two of the Town's three bakers, and an old lady.

One by one (head still masked in burlap, hands still gloved), he dragged their bodies discreetly through the streets and into a shed that his Letter of Introduction had helped him secure. He stacked them neatly on shelves, making sure their arms and feet did not dangle, laboring to minimize the grotesquerie of the job as best he could, putting his training to work. He covered the bodies with blankets and switched off the light he'd worked under, seeing then that it was again dark outside, this time with evening.

He trudged home weary and spent, stopping at the butcher's for a meager cut of lamb and some day-old chicken legs. This was all his hard work had amounted to.

At home, Sarah boiled these in a pot with a dash of salt and part of a carrot, masking her disappointment that there wasn't more, or better. They ate this with a few radishes.

Jakob's hands were so worn from the day's labor he could hardly hold his fork, and he was so tired he could hardly feel the joy he knew the sight of his wife and baby son ought to have sparked in him. That night, after soaking his hands in a bowl of warm water sprinkled with anise seeds, he fell asleep while Sarah was in the bathroom brushing her teeth, and she could not rouse him to make love.

●

**THEIR LIFE CONTINUED** as it had begun. Over the course of that first, lean year, Jakob strangled one hundred and eighty people, including the Postmaster, the Deputy Mayor, eight of the Town's twelve doctors, all of its dentists, seven of its eight Kosher Slaughterers, nine of its thirteen schoolteachers, and all of the neighbors on their street. He even, in what had for a moment felt like a definite step forward, strangled both of the Rival Stranglers who'd been operating in the Town far longer than he had. Neither had ever worked as hard.

All of these he stacked neatly in the shed, which grew fuller by the day. Soon he would need to invest in a new space, or else begin burying the bodies in a field or a pond, practices that his training had taught him to regard as shoddy.

He returned home each night, and together Sarah and he ate their morsels of lamb and chicken, dividing a heel of bread or perhaps a single portion of kasha. They watched the baby grow, his face so full of hope, so full of light and life … though, Jakob couldn't help but fear, shaded also by a cloud of suspicion—the suspicion that life would not meet his expectations even if he lowered them, that life could never give the man what it had promised the boy.

Still, though, day in and day out, they persevered. Jakob came home and soaked his hands, watching the tension ebb out of the knuckles that had strangled so tirelessly all day long, and, together with his wife and child, and a new baby on the way, they prayed to the Almighty. On some nights, they believed their prayers were heard, and, if not answered, at least taken under consideration, along with their many humble good deeds. On these nights, Jakob slept easier, flexing his hands under the sheets, gathering into them from On High the strength to wake into a new day, set out before dawn with his lunch packed, and do it all over again, until the moment—distant still but inevitable—when every last soul in this Town was strangled and stacked, and then their lives would truly be in the Hands of the Almighty, Hallowed be His Name.

# Entry III: The Amateur Funeral

**P**ATKA ESTERHAZY, an extravagantly wealthy widow and Dodge City's primary Krasznahorkai Translator, died at 4 a.m. one miserable morning in midsummer.

There were several Translators of Krasznahorkai from the Hungarian in Dodge City in those days, this being a Town that did things for itself, but Esterhazy, reputed heiress to the so-called and much-discussed European Fortune, had, over the past two decades, easily emerged at the fore of that pack, both for the elegance of her English renderings and for the sheer stamina of her method, which often involved producing several versions of each of the dauntingly dense works of the, as Susan Sontag once put it, "contemporary Hungarian master of apocalypse who inspires comparison with Gogol and Melville."

The only competing Translator of any note by the time of her Death was a beer-bellied single dad named Tom O'Brien, whose mastery over the Hungarian language was called into question after his translation of *Satantango* emerged with the title *Under the Volcano*.

In any event, not only did Esterhazy's passing render uncertain the fate of Krasznahorkai's future translations, but also, more urgently, that of the European Fortune, which had spent the better part of the last century tantalizing Dodge City's romantics.

If her Will was to have any say, it would go to her "milquetoast descendants" but only if they "find the dregs of character in their desiccated-husk-collapsed-honeycomb-hivemind to embalm, bury, and consecrate me themselves. No pros of any kind are to lay a finger on me—that includes you, Professor Dalton. I want them to touch Death firsthand. I want them to have to see it and smell it and be there with it all the way. No delegating this time, nancies. No phoning it in. Try not to take the easy way for once, pantysmears."

Until then, also according to the Will, the Fortune was to be packed into a giant burlap sack and suspended by a crane arm from the courthouse over the Town Square, hanging like an anvil, so that the people of Dodge City might walk beneath it, staring up, waiting for manna to fall.

●

**A FEW DAYS** went by, the body putrefying in the bed where it was found, as her milquetoast descendents searched their hivemind for the courage to do as she'd asked. They bickered and sniped, hiding each other's pills and spreading rumors about one another online.

Townspeople lingered outside her house, with its pretty yellow rose garden, while the crew from *Unholy Family* set up and wandered around with their gear, eating constantly, saying little into the mic, though they were live. The days grew hotter as they waited, smelling the body, hearing the infighting, losing their appetite.

Needless to say, the pros in The Dodge City Funeral Industry stepped in, beseeching them, "Let us take care of this; c'mon, the European Fortune will just go to the Town," but things weren't about to get that simple.

Rumors started up, some involving the possible fraudulence of the Will, others about Esterhazy's long campaign of intimidation and abuse toward her milquetoast descendants ('And who are they, anyway,' the rumor mill wondered, 'the polymothered kids of some alcoholic brother who died in a border skirmish? An adopted gaggle?'), and still others spun tales of older men, Drifters, who may have fathered children with the widow, some aborted, some exposed, and perhaps some about to emerge from the Outskirts demanding their share.

It was said that she forced her descendants to clean her septic tank, forced them to eat expired, unlabeled food from her barely-functional fridge, forced them to lick pus from her caving-in joints for hours on end ... that she trapped them for days in a closet alone with the ink, ink, ink black Heart of

Krasznahorkai's Literary Enterprise, which, it was also said, she had so deep in her possession that Krasznahorkai, himself, had to call her to request permission each time he wished to use it.

In any case: infighting, putrefaction, putrefaction, infighting, grubbing over the Fortune that hung over Dodge City, for days and days and days on end.

●

**THEN**, finally, the milquetoasts found it in them. The Amateur Funeral took place on a Monday, for fear that Sunday might strike her ghost as too professional.

Everyone came out to see it. It took place not in a church or a graveyard, but on the grounds of what had been set aside as a paint factory before the High Priests determined that everything in Town had already attained its Final Color. The partially laid foundation would thus serve as the gravesite, with chunks of broken concrete to hold the body down.

It looked as though her milquetoast descendants had sucked her innards out with an air mattress pump set to deflate. Slumped in on itself, the body looked dry and hungry, wrapped partially in cellophane and partially in tin foil, with what looked like a strip of an old T-shirt covering its neck, which perhaps one or all of them had tried to saw through before thinking better of it.

The milquetoasts—five of them were present, with rumors that two or three more had stayed home, crying in the shower—brought it to the pit on a dolly, and, in front of everyone, tipped it in as unceremoniously as possible.

It landed with a dusty thump. Looking down, everyone could see patches of makeup and lipstick rubbed at random across its face under the wrapping, a couple of barrettes jammed into its hair, a Q-tip in one ear.

Then came the eulogy. The milquetoasts took turns reading from a Good Book they had clearly produced the night before, or even that morning. It looked like a pile of stapled-together printed pages and some notecards and napkins, containing a combination of made-up-sounding Hungarian phrases, fortune cookie aphorisms, alien abduction reports, and an assortment of recent news snippets and multivitamin reviews.

When they'd finished reading, they threw concrete chunks and a tire on top of the body, so that she looked like a witch crushed under a house.

Everyone nodded solemnly, but the milquetoasts enjoined them not to—again, too official. So they tried simply to feel weird instead, to feel no way in particular with none of the feelings about Death they were accustomed to having or had always expected to have when the time came.

Some even claimed that the actual Krasznahorkai, ever the gentleman, appeared at the edge of the scene to lend his singularly uneasy presence to the proceedings, though this, like so much else about the life and legacy of the Great Hungarian Master, was later disputed by Tom O'Brien.

Once the Amateur Funeral was complete, everyone processed to the Town Square to watch the milquetoasts disgorge the European Fortune from where it hung, hoping to catch a stray forint or two borne sideways on the wind.

**I CLOSE** the book, skipping over the comments and addenda sections at the end of each chapter, and leave the Library after this entry, having reached my saturation point. I'm convinced that my sense of the currents running beneath the collective psyche of Dodge City has been enriched enough to get me through the summer. By next fall—how long have I been here?—I'm determined to reopen the question of moving on, this time in earnest.

## Summer of Son of Suicide Sam

**S**UMMER GOES fast. Big Pharmakos drops by my Room intermittently. When I happen to mention my reading of the Folklore, he begins imparting more of it, stories which, he claims, are too raw for print, their meanings still too unstable.

Back in the 70s, he tells me, long before the Suicide Cemetery, there was a spate of a certain type of Suicide in Dodge City. A hard-to-sort type, as the story goes, because it wasn't unanimously clear whether these Suicidees were in fact Dead. They were still present in Town, though they kept to themselves.

This began when, one summer, a figure called or calling himself Suicide Sam either came to or arose from Dodge City.

What he did was approach people, in broad daylight, and whisper, near enough for them to smell his breath, "Now you may, as do most people, have until now shrunk from serious consideration of the prospect of Suicide because of your perfectly reasonable reluctance to undergo pain, gruesomeness, agony, suffering ... "

He had their attention.

"But what if I were to tell you that you—*You!*—could commit Suicide right here and right now with no strings attached, no Blood spilled nor organs ruptured, and, best of all, no effort or patience required?" He'd pause, then continue, "By which I mean, would you give it all up if it didn't hurt?" He'd wave a hand suggestively, a calculated mixture of menace and enticement. "Think about it ... no more tedium, no more fatigue, no more not-enough or way-too-much ... no more worry about next things or the proliferating failures of the past."

Suicide Sam got a number of yesses.

When he got a yes, he simply touched the consenting man, woman, or child on the shoulder, and said, "There it is. All done. Welcome to Suicide."

By July, he was to be seen walking around Dodge City with a gaggle of Followers, all of whom were careful not to talk or respond to or even look at any of the living they came in contact with, especially not their own former friends, lovers, colleagues, families, pets, et al.

Those lines were cut. If they ate, slept, or attended to any other functions of life, they did so in private. No one knew where they went, only that they could not be gotten-through-to. By August, they'd disappeared for good.

●

**"SO MUCH** for the past," Big Pharmakos concludes one morning, as we eat donuts by my window, "except to say that, somewhere in all this, Suicide Sam fathered a son." He continues, "Now, this summer has fast become the Summer of Son of Suicide Sam. I see him all over Town, propositioning people with the old promise of 'No-Step Suicide,' touching them on the shoulder like his father supposedly did, shutting them up for good. They fall into step behind him, hanging back, not making eye contact, while he works his game. He's propositioned me several times. I always rebuff him, saying, 'If it comes to that for me, I want it to hurt, so I can know what it is.'"

He shudders at the thought and shows himself out.

●

**TRUTH BE TOLD**, I've seen him around the streets, too. By August, however, he's retreated, and his Suicidees have begun proselytizing on their own. They've broken with precedent.

Some say this new crop of Suicidees is nothing but a Band of Rebels, aimlessly stirring up anarchy that will buckle under its own weight by autumn. But others see a more darkly religious aspect in it, something beyond the small-time cult trouble we're by now used to.

"Son of Suicide Sam is a darker horse than his dad," is a popular phrase of late.

The Suicidees come right up to you and, their breath awful and copious, whisper, "Do you wanna come back to my place, and … you know?" Always like that, with no variance in inflection or tone.

They're good at finding you, too: they've cornered me in every restroom in Town, even the one-person kind that I lock on my way in.

Most controversial about this solicitation is, of course, the final "you know," since, well, we don't know. There are those who believe the line is simply a rephrasing of the old No-Step Suicide Offer, but these tend to be the types who aren't in the habit of putting too fine a point on things.

Others believe it to be a classic Murder Pickup Line, and are correspondingly wary. Yet others—those who give no credence to the possibility that these people are legitimately Dead—hear the line only in its obvious sexual register.

Needless to say, any requests for elaboration from the Followers of Son of Suicide Sam are met with silence or, at most, the exact same line repeated.

●

**THESE ARE THE CIRCUMSTANCES** afoot when, early one August evening, one of them approaches me in an ATM stall and asks, "Do you wanna come back to my place and watch some Porn?"

I'm so thrown by the variation on the familiar theme that I don't reply.

"Both genders," he adds.

The thing in me that makes me do things makes me nod. "Okay," I say. Something about the concreteness and the clarity of the question—after such a vague summer, I feel not at liberty to say no. Like I might never get another chance to alter my life's course simply by saying yes. This is how they get you, I think.

We walk past the defunct stores, the weed-cut parking lots, the cars on cinder blocks, the empty billboards, the depots where nothing is any longer delivered. Piles of metal parts, piles of fur and rubber, piles of sawdust and stripped paint, and the Bus Station I arrived at, with its smudged Departures and Arrivals Board.

This looks like the territory I worked in when I was on the work crew, though I can't be sure. "Soon we'll be close," he says, and I realize it's the first time he's spoken since the initial query.

●

**AFTER A LOT MORE SILENCE**, we get there. It's an en-campment in a dry riverbed. People are standing around, gawking, moving in a reduced and restricted way, busy with-out it being clear how.

This, apparently, is where the Followers of Son of Suicide Sam are living. Or if *living* is too fraught a word, then *staying*. There are younger and older ones, and, as promised, both genders. The older are, apparently, the crop that the original Suicide Sam culled in the 70s. There are bulky dirt-covered forms all around, in the shapes of trees, huts, animals, but with no defi-nition, all equally dusked.

There is certainly no fire or smell of cooking food, or, for that matter, smell of human waste. I get very cold very fast. There are no chirping crickets or garter snakes whipping around my toes.

There's nothing to say except, "Okay, so where's the Porn?"

Of course, whoever led me out here is nowhere to be seen. He's melded back in among his fellows, just as Dead as they are ... as Dead as, apparently, I am, too. I can't even distinguish people from background shapes like rocks and metal anymore, though I try to hold onto the idea that I'm not alone.

I'd say, 'I took a moment to process what'd happened before moving on,' but, suddenly and for the first time, I feel no hurry to get to things. No pressure to deal with them. I sit down and think, Maybe in a hundred years, maybe in a hundred thousand, I'll stand up, or shift my sitting position ever so slightly. The fifteen minutes I was afraid to waste on my first night here feel redeemed a thousand times over now.

# PHASE VI:

## *The Desert*

# *Internethead's History of*
# *The Dodge City Genocide*

**I**'M WANDERING BACK to Town now that the cold of the Suicide Sam encampment has grown unbearable. No one has tried to prevent my leaving, though no one's showed me the way, either.

I find myself reminiscing on the day in 2007 when Bergman died along with Antonioni. I'm trying to remember where I was when I got the news, and trying not to panic when I find I can't.

Next thing I know, someone's beside me. He tells me his name is Internethead and claims that he's the only man alive who's made it to the End of the Internet. "Just as you would a list of Names," he says, "or a series of Chemo sessions."

He goes on to say that he's now ready to dive back into the Flesh Pool.

I take a step away from him.

"Ha," he says.

His head bulges, especially in the region of his left eye, as though a second head were in the process of bursting up and out through the first. The sight of it makes me think of the phrase 'the son is the father of the man.'

He displays, I realize, the exact symptoms of the New Flesh from *Videodrome*, as if the whole Internet amounted to no more than what VHS and TV, in the end, amounted to.

He's a character cribbed literally from Cronenberg, without even minor adaptation or reinterpretation, like an actor made up to star in one film who, because shooting wrapped early one day, wandered across the lot and onto another set and slipped into the shooting of a completely different film, in exactly the same role, to everyone's apparent satisfaction.

●

**PULLING ME OUT** of this reverie, he says, "You know the little-known story of The Dodge City Genocide?"

I admit that I do not.

"Well," he says, his bulge fulminating, "it was one of the worst."

I can tell that we're walking away from Town now, on our way somewhere new.

"It was," he says, "an untraceable Genocide, as the worst ones always are. No visible bodies, no one to say for sure that it happened. But if you want to talk about Flesh, as I do, you can't ignore it."

My silence inspires, or at least permits, him to continue.

"In the middle part of the last century, some elements came to power in Dodge City that set about purging the Town of what they rather cruelly termed *Ghost Detritus*. They were heavily influenced by the theology of the German Judge and mental patient Daniel Paul Schreber, who wrote endlessly and, for them, convincingly, about, depending on which translation you use, a highly undesirable demographic of *Floating Trash People*."

Internethead buzzes and shivers in a way that I'd describe as Nearing the Edge of the Human. Then he goes on:

"This element turned its dark attention to the equivalent demographic in Dodge City and set about radically exterminating it. The thing is, this Ghost Detritus left no record. Their bodies—living and Dead alike—do not show up in photographs. There is no record of their ever having possessed residences or objects of any kind ... families, jobs ... no trace. So, you won't be surprised to hear, this Genocide has been especially easy to Deny. Even easier than most."

We're standing beside a car now, and I know it's only a matter of time until Internethead tells me to get in.

"Indeed, most of the citizens of Dodge City, if you ask them about it, will manifest no difficulty in Denying that this Genocide ever, in any form, occurred. 'The chill of Ghost Detritus drifts naturally in and out on the winds of history,' is the most you're likely to hear on the topic."

'Aw, I bet you say that to all the Towns,' I want to tell him, but he has a gravity that's hard to interrupt. It's hard to know whether a man who's made it to the End of the Internet ought to be the first or the last one you listen to.

Now he's opening up the car, dabbing his bulge with a handkerchief. He might be trying not to cry. "Get in," he says, and I do.

Then he says he's going to drive me way out into the Desert to see what remains of the Corporeal Victims. "You will not, I promise, feel like Denying what happened after you've seen them."

I initially express concern about being driven 'way out into the Desert' by him, but he just laughs and says, "Man, where I've been, I've seen and done it all ... all I ever wanted to do and then some. It's out of my system."

He makes a fluttering motion with one hand, to show that whatever had been in his system and that I'd been afraid might pose a threat to me has turned to vapor and floated off.

"Sorry about the mess," he says, indicating the Chipotle bags on the passenger seat.

# *Into the Desert*

**I**NTERNETHEAD drives fast, with little apparent regard for the terrain, like he thinks he's still careening from one website to the next. Soon we're well beyond the highway entrance and the cluster of signs that tell you what fast food and motels to plan on when coming to Town for the first time. We pass a Dairy Queen whose parking lot marquee reads: "Another Day Too Sad For Words: $1.99."

I can tell this was the last establishment on the way and wish we'd stopped for a shake. The dark miles beyond feel like discovering new hours in the night, the first time you stay up later than you ever have before and realize you can just keep on going.

Internethead's face bulges peacefully, not showing off for anyone. It's made its point. It may still burst, but it will do so humbly, because it needs to, not because it needs me to believe it can.

Things for the moment are oddly boring, like Internethead and I have known each other a long time and now we're just logging the middle miles among millions. Occasionally I'll point something out and he won't respond, and then he'll point something out, not expecting a response from me.

We get off one road after another ... It seems we're always getting off roads and never onto them, though we go on driving.

A vintage Sparklehorse song plays five or six times in a row on the radio, the reception getting steadily worse. It feels rigged, like the same song is playing again and again to make a point about how much further from Town we're getting, as if otherwise it would be lost on me.

**WE ARRIVE**.

We pull up a steep hill, all gravel and loose dirt, requiring some fancywork with the brakes and steering wheel, and come to a stop in a cloud of dust.

It settles. We wait. Internethead's bulge bulges. I play through a quick memory of a night at the Bar with Big Pharmakos when some teenagers pulled knives on us and we each sidled behind the other, then denied it.

Then we're out of the car, standing up, coming through a free-standing ranch-style gate as a big man ushers us in. Closing the gate behind us, he checks the driveway to make sure we weren't followed.

Once inside, I realize, unambiguously, who it is: Suicide Sam, or Son of Suicide Sam, who, this far out, might be the same guy. Suicide Same, I decide to call him, on the assumption that the father and the son are synonymous here in the Desert. The idea that distance eventually comes to equal time has never felt more obviously true.

"Hi," I say, suppressing any desire to ask whether I'm actually Dead.

He smiles. Internethead and he appear to know one another from a venue other than this one.

We begin to stroll. The air is thick as hamburger grease.

The whole place looks like a long-disused TV set, or one for a show that was never made. It's a patchwork of a place, equal parts 'gone to seed' and 'imbued with a vision so diabolical it could not be realized.'

There are spotlights set up at intervals, dim, like they have no off switches so have been on for years, lost in the blazing sun before coming, feebly, into their own at dusk.

●

**FOR A WHILE**, we were moving through tangible human constructions—ranch buildings, dog kennels, fencing, arrays of tires and engines—but now we're in open Desert.

The air gets even thicker, and I can see Internethead's bulge attain a new closeness to popping.

Just pop, I wish in its direction. It responds by bulging even further, like an ear stretching out to hear my mind.

Now the air's so thick we can barely move, like in those flying dreams that feel more like swimming through a soupy, all-surrounding Substrate.

"Feel that?" asks Internethead.

I admit that I do. I reach out to wipe my arm and pull away a thick smear, which only proliferates as I rub one hand against the other.

Suicide Same is looking away from us, like he's going to say his piece later on.

Internethead continues, "Here's your Ghost Detritus."

He looks at me through a film of air so thick it's almost a crowd. "Here's where they all ended up. This is what the Genocide turned them into ... Ghost Porn, the way of all Flesh."

I had until this point suppressed the feeling, but now I can't: the charge in the air is erotic. There's a crackly, arousing live-ness, or litheness, everywhere.

Internethead looks at me, and I'm ashamed to realize that he knows I'm feeling it. He smirks.

It's cloying all over my skin—an encroaching, densening, slimy, good-feeling influx of Ghost Porn.

I try again to scrape it off—it's thicker than dish soap now—but my hands are trembly, and the pads of my fingers feel huge, magnified out of usefulness. The memory of my Dead Hand aches like a war wound.

So I let it flood me, smearing itself all over my body. A totally disembodied, objectless Pornography. Could be worse, thinks a certain non-trivial part of me.

"Could be much worse," replies Internethead, his bulge now shamelessly engorged.

●

**SUICIDE SAME** turns on another spotlight, this one apparently mounted with an off switch. The Desert comes alive with Pornography. It's everywhere, in all directions, gnashing itself into a fit.

"The fate of all ghosts," he says with a smile.

"Porn sets in the deep, deep Desert," mutters Internethead. I've started to distrust his voice, as I'm no longer able to determine whether it's speaking to the world at large, through his mouth, or straight into my mind, through his bulge.

I've lost a friend, I think.

●

**"ALMOST THERE,"** says Suicide Same, after the spotlights have burned out. Internethead has disappeared, coinciding, it would seem, with my renouncing him as my friend.

"Almost where?" I ask, but too late: it's clear that we've arrived at a hut.

"Prepare to make a new friend. Go knock on that door."

"Why don't you?" I ask.

"He wouldn't hear me," Suicide Same replies, gravely. "He's Dead."

No point in stalling, I think, so I go up and knock on the door. No answer. I knock again, already preparing to knock a third time.

# *A Suicide Note with One Exception*

**O**N MY THIRD KNOCK, a very disheveled boy opens, looking me over with great fondness and relief. Disturbed, I glance away and back at Suicide Same who, clearly, cannot see him.

"What is this?" I ask.

Suicide Same smiles, rubbing the Ghost Porn on his face. "He's yours. Committed Suicide not long ago. Stipulated in his Note that you'd be the only one he'd remain alive to."

I look back at the boy, and it's clear that he can't see or hear Suicide Same. I feel unwell, stretched like this between two mutually exclusive beings, forced to mediate.

"He what?" I ask.

Suicide Same hands me the Note:

> *Dear Drifter whom I met once at the ice cream shop and who was kind to me there,*
>
> *It is with great sadness that I inform you that, on one of my subsequent reprieves from the Dead, I, too, committed Suicide. Who knows why? Perhaps it was simply to take matters into my own hands—to die of my own volition, rather than that of my future adult self. Or perhaps, more simply still, I'd grown weary of the action of coming and going from the Dead, and wished to arrive at a fixed location and remain there. In any event, I am well and truly Dead now, to a degree that I was not before.*
>
> *But, as I would very much enjoy meeting you again, I write this Note in hopes that we might arrange to cross paths with one another on the Plane of the Living. In the Deep Desert, perhaps.*
>
> *Sincerely,*
> *The Boy Sparklehorse*

I fold the Note in my pocket, then look at the boy again, feeling a tear pool in my left eye.

"It's never too late to make a new friend," demurs Suicide Same, before disappearing into the dark. The Ghost Porn sighs as it receives him.

●

**SO NOW IT'S JUST ME** and the Boy Sparklehorse, Dead to everyone else. Maybe he can be my son, I think, looking him over.

# Deeper into Desert, Deeper into Movies

**T**HE BOY DOESN'T OFFER any further explanation of his Note, and I don't force the issue.

It seems clear that the thing to do is to wander on, however aimlessly. If we escape this Desert, it will be because of time—our having spent enough of it here—and not because of space—our having made it all the way across.

So we set out. I hope this means some celestial clock has begun ticking.

As we walk, he starts extemporizing about someone called 'Bob Preston,' and how, if he'd somehow found a way to keep his adult self alive, he may well have met him, perhaps even played and recorded with him, a lifelong dream.

I'm about 85% certain he means Bob Dylan, but I'm wary of correcting him ... warier, I think, than I thought I'd be. Though he seems docile enough, he has an edge of menace, as if his numerous crossings between Life and Death have not only perverted his soul but imbued it with a sort of latent strength that I, by no means, wish to see activated. So I keep my distance, nodding whenever he pauses.

**DAYS PASS**, both of us heavily under the influence of wherever we are. We've managed to snack, but now thirst gets us in a real way.

Perfect timing: a well opens up.

"A mirage," says my son—as I've begun to think of him in my delirium—but he's wrong.

This time, I'm not afraid to tell him. "This time, I'm not afraid to tell you you're wrong," I say.

"Tell me what?"

But it doesn't matter. We've made it to the edge of the water.

We look into it.

●

**AS IT TURNS OUT**, we're both wrong: it is neither a mirage nor a well. It is a deep, deep pit, filled with water. It's about the width of a manhole, the water level just a foot or so beneath the lip of Desert sand it's punched into.

We get on our bellies and lean over.

Peering in, we see that it's stuffed with bodies, floating single file the way they say climbers rack themselves up the steepest, iciest slopes of Mt. Denali.

Looking down, I can see the top of one head and the insinuation of a great many more bodies beneath it.

The funny thing is that the topmost one is not at the surface of the water, the way a floating body seems like it ought to be. There's a full body-length of unoccupied water-space above it.

I feel my ectoplasm jiggle at the sight.

At this point, my son, who doesn't appear to be looking where I'm looking, offers the following: "That's where the Corporeal Victims of The Dodge City Genocide went." He pauses, giving me a chance to look, though I've been looking all along.

Then he goes on to describe the nature of these Corporeal Victims, whose spirits he's encountered in the form of Ghost Porn since ending up alone in this Desert, waiting for me to arrive. A tone of shame creeps in, like the fact of there being Corporeal Victims at all is something he wants to downplay.

He dips his foot down into the space at the top of the water, the space reserved for him. Without his having to say it, I understand that's what the body-length between the surface and the topmost body is ... and I wonder if, for everyone else in the world, for whom he's Dead, they would see a body there already. Perhaps it's only me who sees an empty space in this Mass Watery Grave (MWG).

I feel, without knowing why, hugely glad that this empty space is there. It seems like, if the MWG were full, some awful circuit would be completed—some switch flipped, a horrible machine sprung into action.

I wonder about all the victims of the Funeral of Harry Crews, whether they were Suicides or not, eaten as they were by the snakes they fed themselves to. I don't claim they ended up here, but I don't rule it out, either.

"If this Grave were full," I say, and he shushes me so hard I can tell he knows what I mean.

●

**MUCH LATER**, after we've recovered from the MWG (We both sipped a few mouthfuls from its surface area, to ward off terminal dehydration, and moved on, without his getting in.), we come upon an encampment.

It strikes me as similar to the Depression-era encampment I passed through on my way back from the City of Motel 6s. The air of fading Movie glamour is the same.

"This is where the *Unholy Family* extras live," my son tells me. "There's a law in Dodge City that says that everyone who auditions to be in an episode has to get the part. Labor Dept. put it on the books in the 60s. So the Directors either have to choose the very first people who audition and turn everyone else away, or, as is more common, make hundreds upon hundreds of iterations of the episode, all with different casts."

What we're standing in now is the run-off or longterm effect of this policy. There's trash everywhere, people shuffling around, reciting lines they haven't quite memorized or that haven't been written yet, a few very old and exhausted-looking Directors patrolling the human stew.

My son and I have the feeling of cattle drovers stopping in a rare Town along our route to barter for supplies and to get our equipment worked on before another season in the wild.

One of the Directors comes up to us, looks us over, a glint of hope in his eye. Then he mumbles, "Oh, forget it."

●

**OUR NEXT STOP** is a tableau in which a 10-year-old boy sits alone watching 70s-style pro wrestling on a TV atop a sand dune.

The TV is on mute, sunk halfway into the sand, and the boy is utterly glued to it.

Nearby is a bed with two middle-aged bodies.

This jogs a memory: earlier today, my son told me that his one joy, as a young child, was to watch regional wrestling on TV at midnight on Saturdays. If he was on his best behavior all week, his parents would let him watch in their bedroom (the one TV in the house), on mute, while they slept.

"By parents, do you mean me?" I ask.

He smiles. "That was the 70s, man. A lot of things were different."

I wonder who Sparklehorse's parents were, back in the 70s when he was still Mark Linkous and things were different.

We look at the tableau, posed here in the Desert by one of the Directors, hustling children in and out to make sure they all get a chance to play the scene while the wrestlers on the TV change constantly, as well.

# Suicide Same's Rejects

**W**E PRESS ON after my son takes a turn before the TV.

As we go, we debate the relative merits of the noun *Wanderings* and the verb *wandering*.

It seems to me that *Wanderings* is the less-daunting choice because it's more finite, like an itemized list of tasks that could be accomplished rather than a pure and potentially endless state of being.

"Sure," my son replies, and I can tell he's mentally revising his Suicide Note to name someone other than me as his father.

Well fuck you, too, I think, though I don't mean it and hope he doesn't think I do.

●

**ALL ALONG**, the Ghost Porn has kept crackling, the soundtrack of the rippling heat. It's the only thing happening until we run into Suicide Sam, or Son of Suicide Sam, whom I remember I've rechristened Suicide Same.

There's no real segue: it's just my son and I, bored and dehydrated and starting to bicker, and then it's the three of us in a sort of orchard, surrounded by hanging forms somewhere between meat and vegetable, not quite artificial-seeming but a far cry from organic.

Suicide Same appears either to have been expecting us or to have achieved a state of unshakeable indifference. In either case, it appears he's now able to see my son. "I was just pretending before," he says, revealing that he can now also read my mind.

We end up inside a subsequent cordoned-off area with him, like a crime scene where both crime and investigation are simultaneously in progress.

Soon we're drinking warm glasses of Pepsi and eating crackers and nuts, careful not to touch Suicide Same or to let him touch us, since we all know where that leads.

Once we're refreshed, he shows us the premises.

My son and I have seen so many half-formed, notional places lately that it'd take a lot to make an impression on us.

This place does:

The orchard is stuffed with tangles of skin and bone and exposed muscle, monsters worse than any Western Deity ever protected its Faithful from or leveraged in threat against them. A true free-for-all of reek and malignity.

"The ones I couldn't get right," Suicide Same explains once we've looked as much as we can. "And the ones that wouldn't work with me," he adds, careful not to undersell himself. I think momentarily of the Night Crusher, despondent. This is the man he wishes he were, I think, not without compassion. "The Suicide Cemetery wants nothing to do with them. Says they're not fit for burial. Even for the outermost plots, with the Aberrant and Non-Genre Suicides." He shakes his head, like the thought of exclusion from the Suicide Cemetery is too ignominious to contemplate for longer than it takes to mention.

"I only come out this way once a month. Routine upkeep. Make sure they don't get even stranger, as they have a way of doing when I'm not around. And," he goes on, "I use it for practice. Like a shooting range. Work on my Technique ... the finer points, the kinks that need ironing ... debut new moves. The thing most people don't get is that, to be a True Master at something, you have to remain a True Student of it. Always."

He clears his throat. "When I'm feeling rough, I like to indulge in a little Bodily Improv." His hands protrude from their long sleeves here, showing off a handsome framework of Suicide Musculature, buffed to a sheen after years of work. He holds them out, stretching them open and closed, not quite threatening—we all know he can do whatever he pleases to us—just enjoining us to admire what he's made himself into.

So we do. He's clearly transcended a Limit of Mastery that most people never even reach.

●

**THE SCENE IS ABOUT TO GO ON** too long when a new arrival spares it that fate. Seeing it, Suicide Same nods to us and recedes into a Private Area, pulling a plastic sheet closed behind him.

Evening falls on the rows of ruined shapes, some hardened into their final forms while others seem to be growing subtly, like fruit on a vine.

From among these emerges a child-sized skeleton bedecked in bells and whistles with a wreath around its neck. It stands before my son and me, occasioning a silent spell. Even the Ghost Porn simmers down.

I stare into its hollow skull, its attention heavy on my knees.

In my head I'm calling it a Psychopomp. It's a relative term, inexact, hauled up from some long-ago education I must have received, but it's the best I can do in the moment.

The Psychopomp looks between my son and me, and at the dimming Desert all around us. The crackle of Ghost Porn ceases entirely, and I find that I miss it. Everything's too quiet now.

"It's over," says the Psychopomp. Its voice is that of a very young boy, six or seven, the kind you might try to rope into a choir and castrate.

So I'll call it a 'he,' though it truly is a skeleton, with no gendered Flesh to speak of.

"Seriously, time to go."

My son and I whisper over his head, slowly conferring.

"I can't leave the Desert," my son says. "You know that."

I do know it. "I'm sorry," I say. "I'm glad we got this time together, and I hate to be the kind of father who … "

I choke up, unable to call myself what I know I am.

So we shake hands and part ways. I'm wishing I had some advice or money for him as he vanishes into the rows of hanging Rejects, but the truth is his guess is as good as mine.

Picturing him trudging off to take his place in the MWG, I follow the Psychopomp, who doesn't seem to notice that only one of the two of us is following, unless it was only me he came for.

**I CAN SEE** the lights of Dodge City in the distance. Already I feel my time in the Desert receding into the category of 'boyhood adventures,' which sometimes seem to encompass everything before the present moment, whatever that moment may be.

The Far Outskirts are a Dead Zone. They are silent now, at 3 a.m., certainly, but—the Psychopomp doesn't have to tell me—they're silent all day, as well. They have that air about them. The place feels stained by Silence, stained the way walls are stained with something actually called *stain*, a thing whose purpose is just that.

Almost a show-Town, an ant farm example of how things can end up if allowed to go on and on in one direction with no oversight. Dodge City, it would appear, is surrounded by a cautionary buffer of worse Towns like this, such that, ideally, the best and most central Town is also the one where the realest people live.

●

**"WELL**, this is me," the Psychopomp says a while later, walking up the steps of one of those silent houses. I see him feeling around for the key under the front mat.

By the time the lights of his house come on, I've rounded the corner and reentered the actual Dodge City, where I submit to a relief of return I've rarely before let myself feel.

●

# PHASE VII:

## Back to Town

# The Video Market

I **PASS** the Diner where I first met Gottfried Benn, much closer to Town by this route than by the one I originally took. In the distance, I see the circus power cord lying in the dust, a tiny ridge in the otherwise flat landscape.

I skip breakfast knowing that, if I were in there, I would gladly eat. It's the going-in that I'm unready for. The tinkle of the bell on the door, the KENO cards and gum dispensers, the banality of everything rushing back at me all at once.

Through the window I catch sight of Gottfried Benn and feel my pockets for three 20s, which I don't find. This reassures me that I made the right decision by not going in, though it hardly satisfies my hunger.

●

**I STUMBLE** with my head down into the inner Outskirts, the last buffer zone between here and the Center of Town.

A giant tag sale of VHS tapes, components, copiers, and players is set up in a parking lot. There appear to be no DVDs, though I see a distant table that carries a selection of Laser-Discs and Betamax tapes.

I mainly associate the term 'Video Market' with Robert Rodriguez and how, when he first made *El Mariachi*, he planned to sell it to the Mexican Video Market, rather than using it to become world famous. I've always pictured the Mexican Video Market as a sprawling encampment of folding tables, tents, idling trucks, shredded flags, and guys selling single cigarettes and cans of soda under a wearying sun on a slab of cracked concrete with vultures and snakes rounding the edges, the Border stretching across the horizon.

Miramax kept Rodriguez from that place, but nothing can keep me from it now.

I start picking up boxes, looking at the ratings and the running times, as I have since my thumbs turned opposable. Seeing that big **R** on the back still does something for me.

The LYNCH and CRONENBERG bins are thoroughly picked over; the Video Market must have started before dawn, like a fish market. The containers bearing those Hallowed Names have nothing but ice in them now.

Moving on from this section I arrive at another, less picked over. Finally, I arrive at a bin I can't ignore: DESERT.

There's a subsection marked: DEEPER INTO DESERT / DODGE CITY GENOCIDE.

I work the tapes around in my hands like pieces of athletic equipment or dumbed-down musical instruments, getting their hang. They're unrated and of daunting running times, like 271 mins, two and three VHS tapes held together with rubber bands.

I see myself and my erstwhile son in the pictures on the backs of the boxes. I see Suicide Same and even the Psychopomp, in one of those star-shaped windows they always used to put on the backs of action movie boxes, showing a shootout, a crash, a bloody face or a building in flames.

There we all are.

I surmise one of three things:

1: Someone was filming us the whole time we were in the Desert and hastily cut the footage together while I was returning with the Psychopomp.

2: Someone jotted down everything we said and did, and has somehow already shot a series of reenactments, like on *America's Most Wanted*.

3: Our journey was itself a reenactment of the journeys depicted in these tapes, and thus we are the lookalikes while the actors are the originals.

●

**IN OTHER WORDS**, perhaps the whole journey was canonical, like a Bible story, and we were just one iteration among millions, like Pilgrims on the Road to Santiago, working to convince ourselves that our experience matters beyond serving as one more example of what's already known.

I try to buy up a few copies but can't produce the cash.

●

**THE PERUSAL** leaves me feeling dirty, but I repress this feeling down into my shoes: they, I decide, are the dirty ones.

Putting the tapes back, I drag myself over to where a kid hangs around a shoeshine station. I hunker back at a distance and observe him, and he me. He looks like his mind's gone numb, like he hasn't had a customer all day, maybe for many days.

He hefts his brush from one hand to another; I kick my shoes together, feeling how dirty they are. I want them purged of Desert, polished clean, until no filth of Ghost Porn remains when I reenter the part of Dodge City where people actually live.

The Shoeshine Kid—he looks barely eight; maybe he's a runaway—sees me thinking, surely harder than his customers tend to.

I approach, having decided to tell him, "The usual," and let him take it from there.

●

**I'M IN** the Shoeshine Kid's face, about to say, "The usual," when he panics.

"I'm just not ready!" he shrieks, covering his face with his brush in one hand, his tin of oil in the other, spilling it down his cheeks and nose. "I thought I would be, but I'm not! It's happening too quickly ... It's all happening at once!"

I watch his breakdown and begin to have one of my own:

This scene feels profoundly familiar, not like I've seen it before but like I've always known I would one day, and not just one day, but today ... like my whole life has been a countdown to this, me with Ghost Porn on my shoes, this kid sobbing that he's not ready to give them a shine.

I feel like all I've ever done is kill time until this moment was ready to occur. Like every thought I've ever had has only been a distraction from this one.

I stand back and feel the moment etching itself onto a VHS tape, and know that if I were to go back to the Video Market now, there'd be one remaining copy of *The Shoeshine*, an experimental epic of ambient terror and looming dread, and that the kid at the table would have no choice but to give it to me, once I showed him my shoes and compared them with those on the cover.

Daunted by this prospect—I picture myself watching it alone in the dark, the Night Crusher materializing through the screen to finish me off—I push past the crying Shoeshine Kid and run the rest of the way into Town, praying that, for once, my Room will be ready when I arrive.

# *Big Pharmakos on*
# WTF w/ Marc Maron

**I** **SLOW DOWN** once I reach the backstreets, heading toward Sacrifice Square like I'm surfacing from a high-pressure dive.

Walking through Sacrifice Square, I see my dirty shoes getting dirtier still in an ankle-depth of crushed masks and vials of makeup, gnawed bones, confetti, streamers and smashed piñata material, birds and lizards hatched and trampled quickly underfoot, overturned meat and fried-dough carts, impact dents in the pavement, the familiar ash of burnt effigies, the sticky bandages of homemade mummy costumes, hacked- or ripped-off goat horns and the antlers of other fauna, puzzled over and awl-punctured entrails, spilled gasoline from floats and trucks, and a mess of sleepers who have not yet awakened to begin the appeals process against being considered Dead.

I sit on the lip of the fountain to catch my breath, but soon feel a stirring behind me and turn to see that the water where the carp and catfish used to bathe above the shiny coin bottom is full now of Ghost Porn, crackling like underlit cellophane. It has killed all the fish and repurposed their bodies, opening their mouths and eyes to stare horribly up at me.

They leer, surely aware of who and what I am.

I feel cornered and stand up in a hurry. Trying to regain my balance, I slip and fall in, up to my ankles. The Ghost Porn moans as it sucks the dust and leather off my shoes and into its collective maw, grateful for the taste of Desert.

Barefoot, my skin puckering, I heave myself out onto the cobblestones, crawl to my feet, and run the rest of the way back to the Hotel.

**BETWEEN THE FRONT DESK** and me is a mess of flash-bulbs, the Lobby full of amateur paparazzi and their hangers-on.

I glimpse Big Pharmakos at the convergence of all that camera aim, onstage in the Casino.

"That's right, I've been this Town's Main Pimp and Roughest Comedian as long as anyone cares to remember," he says to everyone writing it down. "But, like, real comedy, you know what I mean? The dark at the end of the tunnel. The leavings and runoff of our species when seen from under the bleachers at Dodge City High."

I can tell he's enjoying skirting the edge of making sense, letting the reporters puzzle it out the rest of the way.

When I get through the circle, he beams: "Where you been, man? I was on Maron's podcast! Went to the garage and everything! Finally my big break, two decades after I'd declared myself a stillbirth. Told my story. How I got to be so funny ... the depths I sank to, the atrocities I committed ... the tissue I shed in my conversion experience. All of it."

Thus the Carnival, I think, picturing the ruin in the streets.

Gibbering Pete pulls me back.

As I'm manhandled out of the crowd, I hear Big Pharmakos say, "Right, and Marc asked me about the Desert, Suicide Same, the Ghost Porn, all my Wanderings ... and I told him, man. I even told him how I left my son. My darkest moment, but I had to do it to save my art from bathos."

The longer I listen, the clearer it becomes that Big Pharmakos has taken my story, wholesale, undigested. Somehow everything I did out there was known to him back here. I flash on the tapes at the Video Market, see all the connections light up, then dim again as I decide not to pursue them. I feel weary and old, my Wanderings long past.

●

**GIBBERING PETE** throws me all the way outside, where it's surprisingly chilly.

I wait a long time, unsure where else to go. Finally, Big Pharmakos comes out. Seeing me, he waves his entourage away so we can talk. My rage at his having taken my story turns to pity. If he wants to live with all that, I think, let him.

"I'm Huge now," he says. "Huge Pharmakos. I'm on the other side of the line."

"So I hear."

"A limo is coming for me anytime," he says, staring longingly at the highway onramp.

"Can I hear the interview?" I ask, not sure if I want to.

He bristles. "It's not up yet, man. I just got a rough tape, and that's for me only. Jesus."

There's a darkness to him that I haven't seen before. The phrase 'rough tape' sounds extra rough the way he says it.

What appears to be a lung blows across the sidewalk and lands on my bare foot.

"People got a little rowdy when they heard the news," he says.

Then his entourage surrounds him, and he's gone.

I take out my phone and search for "Big Pharmakos / Marc Maron." Nothing comes up. I type in "Huge Pharmakos / Marc Maron" … still nothing.

The question of whether Big Pharmakos ever actually went on the show has already become one of those questions you can never ask, like insisting on knowing the personal details of the Historical Jesus instead of just drinking the wine and eating the crackers.

There are times when I suspect that no one in this Town has a working Internet connection. Private Internets, Internets of Misinformation, Internets of Spells and Prophecy, Internets of Rumor and Endless Bifurcation abound, but any link to a system that would allow me to determine the Literal Truth of an event, in the eyes of the outside world, feels heretical even to consider.

I wonder where Internethead is now, how his plan to dive back into the Flesh Pool is working out. Realizing that I haven't yet checked into my Room, I go in to the Front Desk and tell them who I am, or was.

To my relief, like it's taken them all this time to wash the bedding, they say it's ready and I can go on up.

# *The Intestine*

**T**HE FIRST EVENT that grabs my attention after a few calm days is that one night an old man's intestine creeps out his side.

The news report uses the phrase "creeps out" to downplay what must, in reality, have been fraught with a kind of genuine violence, as well as to express the obvious: that it creeps us out, too.

So there he is, a retired tractor mechanic named Murph, pushing 80, sitting in a lawn chair in the Center of Sacrifice Square with a good two feet of intestine pouring out his left side, submerged in a bowl of saltwater on a foldout table beside him.

The cobblestones are still filthy from the Carnival, but not as filthy as they're about to get.

The news report says he came in around sunup one morning, straight into Dalton's home office, the length of intestine bunched up in a pizza box under his jacket. Woke Dalton up, asked to go out back with him, under a drainpipe, someplace private, where he opened the box and showed him what was inside.

"I see," says Dalton, played by a reenactor on TV, coughing into a handkerchief. He leads Murph into Sacrifice Square and props him up with his intestine in a bath of saltwater, then goes home to sleep.

●

**BY DAWN**, the old man's surrounded by almost everyone in Town.

People are taking turns leaning in, hoisting the intestine out of its saltwater, moistening their lips, then sticking it in their mouths to suck out whatever comes.

Murph looks glazed and absent after the first few Sippers take their turns, like once it's been purged of physical shit his body has gone on to offer up deeper and more vital things, from closer to the core.

Of course this only attracts Sippers on a grander scale: the Shit Sipper may be a rare breed, but the Vitality Sipper is nearly everyone. Hundreds of open mouths crowd him like he's a living gas pump or an unlikely source of mother's milk.

●

**IT'S NOT LONG** until a couple of Barkers show up and start charging. Whatever flux Dodge City may be subject to, the nearness of willing Barkers is never in question.

Tickets level off at $35. I get one, though the intestine is clearly sucked out, and I'm not exactly flush with cash.

Murph lolls to the right, away from the intestine, probably wishing he could tear it off without dying.

I step inside the rope the Barkers have set up and do a kind of bellydance as several waves of nausea rock me, one after the other, causing me to retch but not quite spew. I wipe my lips on my collar, then try to fold the collar away from my mouth.

One of the Barkers hoists the intestine out of its brine, shakes the end to dry it off, and hands it over to me. I look at it, greenish-blue and bloody at the end where hundreds of teeth have been at it.

I lick my lips, breathe out through my nose, and stuff it in my mouth.

It's as rubbery as I'd feared, like a tough marinated mushroom, but siltier, like underwater dirt and pebbles, like a frog I chewed once when I was growing up. I breathe in, trying to get a feed going. Nothing but gas comes out. I work its end with my teeth. Murph's groans sound far away. I may be dizzier than I think I am.

I try once more, suck down more gas, swampy as a hot spring, and then the Barkers yell, "Next!"

●

**THAT SOMEONE WOULD** sooner or later fuck the intestine is a given.

When someone finally does, it's almost perfunctory, like he's only doing it because no one else has. Like nature is simply abhorring a vacuum.

That said, though, he's not your ordinary dude. To pick him out of a largish crowd of men as the one most likely to fuck an exposed intestine if given the chance would not be especially difficult.

Outside of Town there's a Peat Bog known as Dead Sir, where we throw the things we want to forget. Sometimes, from the crush of these unwanted things, new things emerge.

Some are vegetal, others human.

Scraping off his body, fully naked, the Dead Sir Drifter appears in Sacrifice Square just after noon on the third day of Murph's ordeal. He approaches the Barkers, hard-on in hand like a credential, and is let through with no request for payment.

Everyone is dazed, weary from the fumes that are basically all that's left in Murph's intestine, but the Drifter's appearance grabs and holds our attention.

He steps up to it, hoisting it out of its saltwater, stretching it open and closed a few times. Murph rolls his head in the direction of what's happening but manages no legible reaction.

The Drifter yawns, then stretches the intestine end even wider and fits it around the end of his cock, working it snug while standing still, rather than holding it still and pushing in.

It takes a moment, but soon the intestine appears to be growing straight out of his groin.

He yawns again, apparently only somewhat invested in what he's doing. He moves back and forth, one hand holding the intestine to keep the seal from breaking.

When he comes, he yawns again, rocking on his heels like he's just awakened and hasn't quite found his balance yet.

Then, still synced up, he stands on his tiptoes and angles the intestine downward, to make sure all the come flows down into it rather than spilling out on the ground when he disconnects.

●

**AFTER THE DRIFTER'S DEPARTURE**, the intestine is left hanging on the cobblestones rather than placed back in its brine bath. None of us has a next move, so we disperse.

But it's not over.

No one wants to touch or go near Murph; I think we all hope he'll just die.

But that's not what happens. What happens is that, after a day, a little nubbin, like a bulb, starts to grow at the end of the intestine. It caps it off, closing the aperture. This growth seems to bring him back to life, and, by noon of the next day, he's calling out for burgers and fries in a voice loud and clear enough that no one in downtown Dodge City can legitimately pretend not to hear him.

So burgers and fries, and a case of Yoo-hoo and a bag of peanut butter cups are brought down and placed within Murph's reach, behind the ropes that the Barkers set up and never took down.

No one can ignore the fact that the end of the intestine has gone head-shaped.

Murph gorges on fat and carbs and, mouth full, bellows for more, which he gets.

We all stand still for several days as the head at the end of the intestine swells further, growing an ass and a torso, and what look a lot like arms and legs, then fingers and toes.

The consistency of the intestine is changing, as well, going whitish and red, losing its blue-green hue. The growth on the end shifts around so that its head is now free and the point of connection is at its belly.

The word *placenta* rises from our throats.

This goes on another day, a pile of burger and candy wrappers surrounding Murph where he sits, the baby growing and growing, eating its way closer to him.

There's a poignant moment near the end where Murph turns his head (which had been averted all this time) to stare at the baby face-to-face, recognizing himself in his offspring for the first time.

●

**WHAT DO THINGS LEAVE** when they're over?

In this case, a baby bawling in a mess of spent placenta atop its Dead parent.

Dalton dons a pair of surgical gloves and steps in to extract it.

# *A Disturbance in*

## *The Dodge City Pornography*

**B**ACK IN MY ROOM, all I can do is watch TV.

The story of burying the new baby in Dead Sir plays endlessly. "To be with its father," claim those who buried it, their voices fraught with doubt. "The baby's father emerged unbidden from Dead Sir, so it's only fitting that this father should now receive his newborn son at home," is the official story. From my Room, however, it looks clear to me that the baby is Dead.

Then this story ends, with no mention of Murph, whom I imagine would have to be considered the baby's mother.

The story that follows is more interesting. It doesn't draw the explicit link between the emergence of the Dead Sir Drifter and the disturbance in our Pornography, but it's clear that some link exists.

Everything, I'm coming to understand, is in service to the new season of *Unholy Family*, which premieres next week. The whole Town is headed in this direction.

●

**TONIGHT'S NEWS STORY** begins as a historical segment on The Dodge City Porn Village. Its nostalgia for the old days of the Village is itself pornographic, basking, as it does, in the dream of a lost perfection, a Harmonious Order from which we are now condemned to wander in exile.

The more I watch, the more I feel myself slipping inside the order being described: the merger from *them* to *me* has a momentum of its own. In this way, the news report is a ceremony, inducting me into The Dodge City Gene Pool.

"The Porn Village," the newscaster explains, "is where the Objects of The Dodge City Pornography were born and bred, living according to some harmonic, inscrutable order of their own, often conceiving and even birthing their next generations in front of the camera, then dying quietly and going to seed.

"The Village keeps to itself, a few miles down a dirt road leading straight out of Dodge City. In the grand tradition of Human Sacrifice, where victims are bred like cows in the Outskirts, fed on special mash and informed of their purpose from Day 1, our Porn Objects breed and are born for us, so that we, too, in our shy manner, might likewise breed and give birth.

"We watch what Porn we're given, one VHS per night. Each of us lives alone, and is in that sense a virgin.

"We insert the tape and watch the screen fill with Objects of all ages and sizes, eating, sleeping, showering, defecating, copulating, sometimes committing Suicide and watching other forms of TV ... all in the nude, or in ripped, too-tight underwear.

"The physical connection between their bodies and our own is just loose enough to be exotic and just tight enough to be familiar (allowing us to believe we can feel what they feel, mapping their nerves onto our own). We recognize ourselves in them, though we also know better than to think we might manage to do what they do, with one another here in Dodge City, without their mediation.

"After we've watched each night's allotment, we put the tape out with the trash before it starts to stink like a container of half-eaten chicken salad.

●

**"DODGE CITY'S PORNOGRAPHY** is not for pleasure. We have, over the course of weakening generations, made it the basis of our Reproductive System.

"Males, on this diet of one fresh Porn per night, save their resultant sludge in plastic bags, which are collected weekly by kids on bikes—the same kids, androgynous and parentless as far as anyone knows, who deliver the Porn itself, serving as go-betweens to the Porn Village.

"These bags are then emptied in a compost pile in the Community Gardens, where their content mixes with itself and with the soil to serve as both fertilizer and pesticide for our produce as it grows.

"When our produce comes ripe in September—a kind of reddish-black ground-meat product, a pre-human Substrate pocked with sketches of musculature—the females of Dodge City convene at the YMCA.

"They dine, then take their Porn into separate rooms, along with their portions of Substrate, and, when they are ready, lit by the grinding, sometimes dying Porn Objects onscreen, they implant it in themselves, as far in and up as it will go, until it takes and begins to gestate, as the tape sputters out with a rancid stench.

●

**"IN JUNE**, the next crop of Dodge City young is upon us, let loose onto the YMCA playground to fend for itself until it, too, develops the taste for Porn, and our species evades extinction once again.

"In this way, our genetics swim in a concentric circle around those of the Porn Village, the two streams touching at certain points but never crossing."

A commercial break, then:

"Research has revealed a longstanding practice in The Dodge City Police Dept. of replacing every citizen it executes with an impersonator culled from its own ranks.

"In tribute," a spokesperson explains, "to each fallen member of our Town's Underclass, without which we would have no buffer between Earth and Hell.

"In the course of time, the Police force shrinks and the Town's seamiest population swells with impersonators, who, naturally, allow the thrill of being 'back from the Dead' to consume them, to the point where, like swapping in fresh flowers for wilted ones, it becomes incumbent upon The Dodge City Police Dept. to execute and replace them once again.

"None of which would've impacted our Pornography had these impersonators not crossed the line, seeping out of Dodge City and into the Porn Village like swamp gas into the Gene Pool, turning it from clear to green.

"But they did.

"'We wanted to feel what it was like,' they've claimed, 'Real Flesh for once. The good stuff.'

"This was a while ago. Since then, their peaceful Incest disturbed, the Porn Objects have been on a course of increasing aberration: shrunken arms, bulging heads, protruding vertebrae, glistening spots on their bellies that look semi-solid, like smears of gel in place of skin and muscle.

"And their genitals: squiggles, nests, blurs, double- and triple-protrusions, and sticky hanging tangles like distressed gobs of putty, interacting with one another in no set way, finding no happy medium or snug fit, only abrading, slipping past, chafing each other, wearing each other down or peeling each other off.

"Procreating in our solitary fashion on this side of what's left of the divide, we have no way of knowing how widely this genital disturbance has spread to the citizenry of Dodge City, contagiously through the Porn we continue to ingest.

"We are disgusted by these images, alone in our nights, and we are riveted by our disgust. We feel our genes shifting, our genitals turning foreign in our hands and beneath our fingers, as we work them over again and again, helpless to keep from perverting them further.

"The serial contact we make with ourselves, indeed, comes to feel ever more like tampering with models that are not yet finished, smudging their emergent design.

"The males still fill their plastic bags, and the kids on bikes still arrive to collect them, sowing the Community Gardens to grow its tomatoey meat, which the females still implant in September and carry until June, but the fear is that this new crop will resemble nothing so much as the increasingly alien Porn Objects that presided over its genesis, all toothy eye-sockets and sealed-up earholes, fused lips and exposed bladders.

"We fear, like every generation fears, that we will, somehow, be the last, having unwittingly ceded our habitat to a new species that will heave us groaning deep into the murk of Dead Sir."

**THE NEWS REPORT** ends after a teaser for tomorrow night's segment, which promises exclusive footage of the original Police Impersonator Rampage. It shows a clip of all those proxy murderers and rapists flooding the Porn Village, loosening their belts to pop its bubble of separatism, stirring the genes that loop and twine through us all in a Walpurgisnacht of hellish abandon.

"All of which, as if we needed to tell you, is shown in the service of building anticipation for the premiere of the new season of *Unholy Family*, airing right after tomorrow night's segment!"

I click off the news and warm up my VCR just as the kid knocks on my door with tonight's Video. When he's gone, I sniff it, pacing around, and taste the tape itself under the plastic flap. Then I put it in the VCR and get my bag ready.

# *At Dead Sir with the Night Crusher:*
# *Goodbye to My Material*

**FTER TONIGHT'S PORN**—my first emission directly into The Dodge City Gene Pool, a step I found myself powerless to resist taking—I fall into a daylong catatonic nightmare.

Fumes from my old Material, my last link to where I came from and only reminder that I came from anywhere, baste my dream-mind with terror. My nightmare buries me in images of my fingers being shaved off until a knock at the door wakes me. Fingerless and still partly paralyzed, I crawl out of bed and hug it open.

There stands the Night Crusher, dressed in a cloth jumpsuit with a black plastic poncho stretched over and lashed around his waist with a bungee cord. He's lanky, but it's belted so tight a few rolls of fat pop out.

"Wet out there," he mumbles, his eyes a dim orange rather than the flaring red I remember. "Been to Dead Sir twice already and it's only—" We both look at the clock to see what time it is. Late.

I'd heard rumors that the Night Crusher was transitioning into a new line of work, but it's sad to see him so diminished before me.

"Turns out I was using up too many people before," he says, twisting a strand of chest hair that protrudes from his poncho's collar. "Crushing them to the point of uselessness. 'We are not exactly in a position to be profligate with our bodies,' Professor Dalton told me not long ago. 'It's not exactly still the Baby Boom around here, if you haven't noticed.' So now I'm more like a recycling man. Repurposing bodies rather than ruining them for good."

I nod and try to act like I think his career change makes sense given the current state of things, though I'm thinking, Are you sure you weren't fired because you were simply too depressed to do your job? How many people did you actually crush, in the final reckoning?

It's nice that he's still working, though, I go on thinking, as if I'm the one who needs comforting. I want to tell him that I was partially crushed just now, but I fear this will only underscore his irrelevance.

As if aware that my thoughts are turning against him, he holds up a cardboard cake box, and I don't need to think very hard to know that my fingers are inside, arranged in two layers of five with ice in between.

Next comes a moment of black humor where he pushes the box toward me with one hand and, holding up one of those digital package-receipt signature machines with the other, says, "Sign here."

We both giggle like, What do we have to lose?

At this point I lose clarity. I know better than to expect to recognize the point at which I am again fully awake. Certainly, the Night Crusher is here for real, and my fingers are gone, nestled nicely in the box he wants me to sign for. But beyond that, I couldn't say.

He explains that his new job mainly consists of making the rounds in the night, gathering up Material to submerge.

Material ... it comes clear to me that it's time to let mine go. It has no value here, and I'm not returning to where it does. Without it, I'll relinquish whatever memory I have left of the place it came from, like a once-great Empire burying all evidence of its Colonies after the Tide of History has turned against it.

●

**BEFORE MAKING THE TRIP** to Dead Sir, we reattach my fingers. I tell him, optimistically, that I can pay for everything at the start of next month. He jots this in his ledger. Then we sit at my bathroom counter and spread all ten out, painting the stumps with superglue like we're applying false fingernails before the prom.

"I only shaved them down a little," he says, consolingly, maybe guiltily.

Once attached, I hold them down by my side and wait for the glue to dry. They feel more like things I'm carrying than things that are me.

●

**I FOLLOW** the Night Crusher out of the Hotel.

Carrying my bags, which contain all the Material I stashed on my first night here, I feel the glue on my knuckles bind with skin flaps and exposed bone. It's dark in all directions, thick with trees until we get right down to the banks. After we push through a layer of cattails, the Night Crusher clicks on a flashlight, revealing the oily expanse of Dead Sir.

"Ready?" he asks.

I hesitate, then nod yes. He turns his back and puts his headphones on to give me a moment alone.

The bags fall from my hands. I watch them break the surface and begin to sink, down to where the intestine's baby is decomposing, and perhaps also growing into a new form, one stranger and stronger and more fit for this world.

# *Blood Drive and Incest Father:*
# *Season Premiere of* Unholy Family

**A**BLOOD DRIVE TENT is set up by the edge of Dead Sir. Others who've been here in the night dumping materials of their own are lying on cots, opening their arms.

Professor Dalton is inside, lecturing about how a fresh audit of our fluids is essential. "A stocktaking, a time to juice ourselves out and see what's afloat in us," he says, sipping orange juice from the sugar-station that's been set up to keep donors from fainting.

The Night Crusher, still wearing his headphones, pushes me inside and says he'll be waiting. I stumble, and then I'm lying on a cot with a needle in my inner elbow, my Blood shooting out through a tube.

I'm swooning hard. The ceiling of the tent looks like one big ceiling fan.

I follow its rotation as the sound of Blood fills my ears, and I see it all running together into a tub in the center of the tent, some lighter red and some almost black, all swirling into a single substance. The tent swells and heaves as all of Dodge City crowds inside, and the needles make exhausted panting sounds.

●

**I PASS OUT** for a while, into a dream of my Material in the black of Dead Sir. When I come-to, the Night Crusher is leading me by the hand into the Diner for a restorative breakfast.

I let him order bacon and eggs for both of us, while I press on the gauze taped to my inner arm.

We eat without speaking until Gottfried Benn shows up. My spine cramps with the awareness that I don't have $60 on me, but it doesn't seem to matter, as Benn's enthusiastically recapping last night's episode of *Unholy Family*, the season premiere, and so has no attention for me.

I listen in.

●

**IT FEATURES** an old man in a mansion in an archaic Mississippi film set, capacious grounds gone to seed, his wife buried out back, three beautiful and slightly insane daughters in Gothic bedchambers.

The old man roams the hallways of his once-great mansion wearing a Chinese silk nightshirt, blue and crimson, muttering, bumping into statues and rotting chests.

Paintings hang crooked from the walls, and the walls themselves sit crooked on their floors, soft as wet cork.

The old man sees Death in every crud-covered window and dusty glass door, taunting him with the baleful wiping-away of his life and its failure to make a mark, even an indentation, on this estate inherited from his father and grandfather and on and on, all more notorious figures than he.

In moods like this he passes his daughters in the halls, drifting in gowns on feet that seem barely to touch the floor, and he plays at pretending he cannot tell them apart, and then wonders, indeed, whether he can.

On one such day, a terminal idea blooms up in him:

I will end my life an Incest Father, surrounded by children who are also my grandchildren, my daughters defiled. A final bid at lasting shame.

There is a long and vaunted tradition of old men implanting in their young daughters the children who will one day inherit the Estate, and one day bury their mothers on its grounds.

Indeed, such is the story of my own parentage, thinks the old man, as if this were a fact he'd long forgotten and just now remembered, in the nick of time.

If I can bring this shame upon myself, I will die with a measure of dignity within the tradition I belong to, he thinks.

●

**SO HE GIVES** it a try.

Starting that evening, after dinner and cocktails, he fucks each of his daughters, each in a different place—pantry, basement stairwell, laundry room—whispering to each not to tell the others, trying to work into his tone a note of threat that she and he both know he cannot back up.

The daughters suffer his incursions with a kind of formalized and ironic disdain, playing at trauma and disgust, aware of the cliché in his behavior, the conformity to stereotype, and of their own stock roles in the classic scandal.

Each pretends to promise not to tell her sisters, and then tells her sisters, and this, too, of course, is part of it.

The atmosphere in the house stabilizes for a while, the old man doing his best to keep his strength and to stay consistent, waiting for one or two or all of his daughters to take pregnant and for the shame-children to start their months-long Southward crawl to fruition.

But it doesn't happen.

He's just too old; he's waited too long, spent too many years wandering in celibate delusion, forestalling the idea he should have had as soon as the first daughter reached puberty.

There is nothing, it would appear, of the genuine Incest Father left in him.

He starts drinking raw milk and eating rare meat at every meal, but his potency will not return. He can hear his daughters laughing at him in the echoes of the house, and it's little more than a mockery, now, whenever he corners one of them and rucks his nightshirt up.

He admits defeat, lies down, prepares to die. He lies there a long time, but Death only stands above the frail old man and says, "Prove to me you're worth taking."

●

**HERE**, at the bottom of his life, the old man uncovers another idea. A last resort, certainly, but an idea, nonetheless.

He sits up, showers, and leaves the house for the first time in a decade. Asks his shed-dwelling groundskeeper to ready the Cadillac and drives to Town, seven miles north on the Memphis road, across a broad tract of reclaimed swampland.

Here, the old man fetches a young man, strong, healthy, naïve. He finds him skulking among the tonics at the back of the drugstore, looking for any work at all. It takes very little to make an arrangement.

Back in the mansion, the old man sits the young man down at the dinner table with his three daughters and explains how it's going to be:

"You will fuck them *as* me," he explains, handing the young man the silk nightshirt to wear, "and they will become pregnant with my children, and I will be a real Incest Father after all, and after I die, you will go into a grave in the basement and remain in there forever, so that my daughters may be left alone in this big house to grow old with these children fathered in shame, losing hold, year by year, of the memory of anyone but their father ... You, young man, will become to them a vague fantasy, a kind of long-lost Incubus ... Any questions?"

The young man and the three daughters shake their heads.

"Then, please begin."

●

**THEY DO**. The house fills with sex-noise, and nine months later four babies arrive: one each for two of the daughters, and twins for the youngest.

The old man calls the Church and says he's dying and would a Pastor please pay him a last visit. The Church says one will be right over.

"Okay," says the old man. "A witness is coming. Ladies, please arrange to be seen with your children. And you," he says to the young man, "are finished here. Please crawl into your grave in the basement."

The young man, though something of a simpleton, appears to understand.

The old man prepares to meet his demise, scorned in the eyes of the Church as yet another Incest Father from a long line of them, a notoriety he's certain he deserves at the end of such a long and lonely life.

The old man begins dying on the divan, and the Pastor comes to his side and opens his briefcase, and the daughters, on cue, emerge with their babies, and the Pastor, also on cue, puts two and two together, whitening with shock ...

But then the young man enters the room, in good cheer, drinking milk from a gallon jug in his boxers, his massively chiseled, tattooed torso in full view, and the lustiness with which the daughters regard him, combined with the degree of resemblance in the babies' faces, reorders the Pastor's assumptions entirely.

"Ah," says the Pastor, relieved. "I didn't know the babies' father was ... at home. For a moment, sir ... " he says, gazing now lovingly at the old man. "Well, for a moment there, I'd wrongly assumed that ... "

●

**AND THUS THE OLD MAN DIES**, from shame, but a genuine rather than a generic shame, a shame of impotence, a true shame that Death cannot expiate, a damning shame, mortally humiliated by the Pastor's Last Rites, said over a dying man whose life has truly come to naught.

When he's buried in the backyard later that day, he is not at all looking forward to meeting his forebears in Hell, all those legitimate Incest Fathers lined up to receive him, wrongly believing he is one of them. He wonders, as the dirt falls on his face and lands in his mouth, whether it will be possible to lie in Hell, or if down there all things are transparent.

●

**AS GOTTFRIED BENN FINISHES** the story, Big Pharmakos—I still call him this in my head, though I know he prefers Huge Pharmakos now—and his entourage come into the Diner. The Night Crusher flees at the sight, and Big Pharmakos hands Gottfried Benn the standard $60 hush money. He pulls it from a money clip with a largesse he's affected since his appearance on *Maron*.

Benn leaves, taking, as ever, a newspaper and toothpick on his way out. It occurs to me, as I see him walking off with that cash, that I should ask him how he does it. If I can get the hang of making $60 at a time, I might be able to build a future here.

Big Pharmakos tells his entourage to wait outside and sits down across from me.

We order pie, though I've already eaten, and he starts talking about the national tour he's just getting back from. "I did a set at the White House," he says. "I played Carnegie Hall." I don't mention that I've regularly seen him hanging around the Hotel, filling a takeout container at the breakfast buffet just before the staff starts cleaning.

I'm thinking about *Unholy Family*, wondering if it's symbolically relevant to my life as it stands now. I try to determine if the predicament of the father, or the daughters, or the young man, holds any clues as to my own best next move, but soon let the strands go.

After Dead Sir and the enervation of the Blood Drive, these seem like old ideas, of academic but not actionable interest. In their absence, it's just Big Pharmakos and me, the day open before us. His entourage is standing outside the window, facing away.

I feel my life puffing up to its full size like something has been pressing it down until now. I can see myself in a few decades sitting in this same seat, defending it against others, demanding they sit elsewhere.

I start to wonder what will be on *Unholy Family* next week, what fresh pulp it will provide for the next morning's chewing, here in this same seat with the same people who are here now.

Then I notice my thoughts turning toward another side of the *Unholy Family* paradigm: not what I'll see next time I turn on my TV, but who's behind it, inside the screen, making what happens there happen. I'm thinking, if I'm honest with myself, about what it might take to get a job. I'm thinking about getting a foot in the door of The Dodge City Film Industry and where that foot, once in that door, might lead the rest of me.

I picture myself moving out of the Hotel—after finally settling the bill that has been growing unchecked all this time—and into some space larger and more fraught than my Room and all the rooms before it. I feel weary and broken down, but, at the same time, excited that a new season of *Unholy Family* has begun, its trajectory still unknown but the force of its impact already palpable in the air. It feels like the beginning of a new season in the genuine, astronomical sense.

I snap out of this when our pie arrives. Big Pharmakos looks like he's been staring at me this whole time, thinking no thoughts of his own. I nod to acknowledge him, drain my water, then pick up my fork with my formerly Dead Hand, looking at the gauze on my inner left elbow as I flex my reattached fingers to scoop pie from my plate.

●

# EPILOGUE:

## *Roll Call; My Incorporation*

**B**IG PHARMAKOS and I walk out of the Diner, bill paid, to mingle with his entourage in the street out front. "Blood Drive Results are in," one of them says. "Let's go hear who's who."

With this, we start walking. As we go, others trickle in from the side streets and out of the Hotel. There's the familiar sense, accompanied by a whoosh-like sagging sound, of Dodge City's interiors emptying out, spilling their contents onto the streets and eventually, as if it were the bottom of a bowl, into Sacrifice Square.

I follow, on the assumption that attempting to flee would only delay the inevitable. No need to claw your way up the bowl's edges only to slip back down, I tell myself, as if I were any kind of authority. As we get closer, I feel the vastness of the world beyond Dodge City shrinking, losing color, ceasing to be much of a world at all. I ask myself where I came here from and picture myself shrugging. I picture all my notes, envelopes, and receipts sinking deeper under Dead Sir, their ink leeching out and melting into Folklore, seeping into The Dodge City Groundwater to filter back up through the stories we tell ourselves and one another in person and on TV.

So I remain with Big Pharmakos and his entourage, all of us blurring into everyone else in Sacrifice Square. Next time I look up, all I can see are the backs of heads and, in the distance, the face of Professor Dalton.

●

**WE FALL SILENT** as he approaches the podium on the stage he's standing on, donning his golden bird-mask and opening his mouth, deep in the beak's shadow. "Hello, Drifters," he begins. "Hello, People of Dodge City, those of you who've made it this far."

He unrolls a parchment that I assume contains the Blood Drive Results. As soon as he begins to speak, whatever chaos has reigned here so far feels like it's resolving into a Power Structure I'm powerless to stand outside of.

The atmosphere feels pregnant, swollen, like something's growing in the sky over Dodge City ... something that, before long, will signal the end of my long bachelorhood and the beginning of a new and possibly terminal domesticity. Whether it's due to my recent congress with the Pornography or to something far subtler, I can't say. Causes, I've often found, remain in shadow even as their effects grow over-whelmingly clear.

Part of me insists it's still not too late to leave, and I notice my feet shuffling on the cobblestones, while Dalton's voice continues in the background. I can make out the words, "Robert ... Stevie ... Layla ... Marianne ..."

What I wonder most is, will the phantasms settle down if I stay? Will they stop, stranding me in normalcy, outing everything I've experienced here so far as a solipsist's hallucination? And do I want them to? Would I rather the life I've lived here continue, or am I ready for a new phase, even if that phase is quiet, calm, work, money, sex, Death, and no more?

As Dalton moves deeper into the Roll Call, matching each set of Blood Drive Results with a name and thus a body—to replace all those the Night Crusher rendered useless, before he changed jobs?—I look over at Big Pharmakos for a sort of reassurance I know he can't offer. His concerns have never been mine, and vice versa, though I also know it isn't nothing to have a friend. If I remain in this assembly, I think, Dalton will eventually get to me. One of the names he reads out will be mine and my body will be compelled to claim it. There will then be no repressing what's in my Blood.

But what else? Drift further, into a new Dodge City, to do it all again, until I reach this same moment there, to wonder again what I'm wondering now? Is that the way to live? Perhaps. Perhaps all one can do is run down the clock, keep ahead of it until it ends, suddenly, without there having been any dread in the lead-up.

Dalton continues reading names, thereby summoning Drifters to kneel before him one by one. I feel my heart swell, ready to be torn from my chest, though I know the reality is the opposite: that something extra is going to be stuffed in, into a space I may or may not have.

"And you," Dalton booms, "you will be called Dylan." A hooded figure kneels to receive the name that will be on his headstone.

Again I try to make a run for it, and actually get a few feet away from where I was, but then I'm overcome by a vision of utter desolation, of the whole rest of the country—and the world, and all possible worlds—turned to nothing, to such pure wasteland that even roaming aimlessly across it is unimaginable. Everything that's anything is present here, in Dodge City, compacted together and turned, by its own density, into a new substance. The question of escape seems beyond blasphemous now, well into the realm of pure absurdity.

I burst out laughing. I fall to my knees laughing. The fact that all of this, any of it, anything at all, exists strikes me as painfully funny. Too funny, dangerously so. My face is on the cobblestones, my tongue in the grout between them, and I'm thinking, Maybe this is how it could be, me the Raving Madman, the Fool, one of dozens or hundreds gibbering into The Dodge City Ground.

●

**WHEN I CATCH** my breath, I let Big Pharmakos, who's laughing, too, help me back to my feet. We laugh together until we have to catch our breaths again.

Then, sobered, licking dust from my lips, I begin to wonder about the line between the consciousness of an *I* and that of a *We*. If I let mine dissolve into a *We*, I wonder what role might it take up, if not that of another madman? I picture the doors of the studio where *Unholy Family* is produced and again see my foot, independent of the rest of me, sliding through, seeking purchase on the, no doubt, slippery tiles inside.

I see myself coming home from work, three 20s in my pocket, no longer to my Room but to a house at the end of a dead-end street, or perhaps the house I once feared had burned down. The house where stasis will finally set in.

But then inside this house, all the way inside, roaming its dim hallways, I glimpse the door of another Room, slightly ajar, a terminal within the terminal, the point where insanity breaks back through, the new *I* buried deep inside the *We*, where surely I'll ...

"And you," Dalton booms over the crowd, cutting off whatever hopeful or fearful thought I might've had next. I know he means me. I'm the last one. "You ... " His voice echoes, hanging over Sacrifice Square before it coalesces into a name.

Whoever I was before, I think, wherever I came from, one second from now all of that will be nothing. Unless I've been here all along, I think, and it's taken me this long to realize it. Then I stop thinking. I close my eyes and see my thoughts smothered under a thick black cloth as I savor the last of my anonymity for all it's worth.

# ABOUT *the Author*

**DAVID LEO RICE** is a writer and animator from Northampton, Massachusetts, currently living in New York City. His stories have appeared in *Black Clock*, *The Collagist*, *Birkensnake*, *Hobart*, *The Rumpus*, *The New Haven Review*, *Identity Theory*, *Nat. Brut*, and elsewhere. This is his first novel. He has a B.A. in Esoteric Studies from Harvard University and is online at: raviddice.com.

# ABOUT *the Artist*

**CHRISTINA COLLINS** is a writer, musician, and visual artist living in Minneapolis. She holds an MFA from the Rainier Writing Workshop and is the author of the debut collection of poetry, *Conspiracy of Beauty*, and a founding editor of *Lockjaw Magazine*.

# **AUTHOR** *Acknowledgments*

Sincere thanks to Leah Angstman, Jeff Jackson, Matthew Spellberg, Jack Ketchum, Simon Pummell, Tim Credo, Isaac Shivvers, Julian Arni, Andrei Cristea, Robert Rice, and to Eli Epstein-Deutsch for his invaluable assistance in the development of this project.

# **COLOPHON**

What you are holding is the First Edition of this novel.

The cover title is a combination of the fonts Ludovicos, created by SDFonts; Gipsiero Kracxed, created by Bumbayo Font Fabrik; and Essays 1743 Italic, created by John Stracke. The vignette headers and dedication are set in Essays 1743, and the phase headers are set in Gipsiero Kracxed. The back cover Alternating Current Press font is set in Portmanteau, created by JLH Fonts. All other fonts are set in Calisto MT.

Cover artwork is by Leah Angstman and Michael Litos. Interior illustrations are by, property of, and ©2016, 2017 Christina Collins, used with permission, and created exclusively for this collection. Find her at yourfriendchristina.com. All rights reserved.

The Alternating Current lightbulb logo was created by Leah Angstman, ©2006, 2017 Alternating Current. The circle graphic was created by Ocal. The scroll graphic was created by Tanya. Christina Collins' photo was taken by and ©2015, 2017 Rachael Conley. David Leo Rice's photo was taken by and ©2016, 2017 Sebastian Siadecki.

All fonts, artwork, graphics, and designs were used with permission. All rights reserved. The publisher wishes to thank all font, artwork, and graphic creators for their generosity in allowing legal use.

# OTHER WORKS

## *from Alternating Current Press*

All of these books (and more) are available at Alternating
Current's website: press.alternatingcurrentarts.com.

alternatingcurrentarts.com

Made in the USA
Middletown, DE
20 January 2019